How They Spend Their Sundays

How They Spend
Their Sundays

stories

Courtney McDermott

Whitepoint Press
San Pedro, California

A Whitepoint Press First Edition 2013

Cover design by Monique Carbajal
Cover photo © iStockphoto.com/gdagys
Author photo by Laura McDermott

ISBN - 13: 9780615793696
ISBN - 10: 061579369X

Library of Congress Control Number: 2013936417

Grateful acknowledgement is made to the original publishers
of the following stories in this collection: "A Bottle Full of
Nothing," *The Daily Palette* (November 2008) and "The Secrets
of Mothers and Daughters," *Sliver of Stone Magazine* (October
2012).

Published by Whitepoint Press
whitepointpress.com

For

My family: Patrick, Laura, Maggie and Quinn

My Peace Corps family

My Basotho family: the Makaras of Maluba-lube
and 'Me Makabi

Contents

Part Three

How They Spend Their Sundays

PART ONE

Fag Hag in Fuchsia

JOHANN

Johann was throwing a dinner party without his wife and sons. Mainly because they didn't know about the party, for Johann had left them to live this other life. He now managed the Sun Hotel in Maseru, close enough to the South African border that he could still smell his old life.

He had picked up the Americans earlier in the day. Cici and Adam he knew from the club, where blow jobs were conducted in bathroom stalls. Heather was a surprise addition. She had dined at the hotel restaurant before, and with her auburn hair, she was hard to forget. She laughed a lot, and though she was straight, she seemed like a good person to invite. This was a party of celebrations, and Johann knew the more people, the better the celebrations. Besides, she was stranded in the city with nothing to do.

Johann crammed the Americans into his car next to his boyfriend Z and Belinda, the petite, homely Mosotho who had lived in England for years and only recently returned with an insatiable desire for women. They drove up the windy road to the Dutch ambassador's house where Johann stayed. Through the hotel he made friends with all the ex-pats and wriggled his way into house sitting for them when they went on holiday.

The guests were a collage of people from Johann's history and present life. They all drank champagne and went through the achingly awkward motions of introducing and reintroducing each other. This is how I know so-and-so and we work together, or we're just together.

The gardens around the pool had been tended with hoarded water, and they shone in waxy greens under the pool spotlights. Spiky red flowers and a pomegranate tree from some other exotic locale pierced the green. Two cars were in the garage and a third in the driveway. A baby grand piano in the otherwise empty music room, and ice in the freezers, things which Johann used to impress Z. Z, twenty years younger than Johann, was thin and beautiful with a large mouth and a round Adam's apple. He wore a pink shirt, sleeves rolled up, and crisp white pants and sandals he had kicked off. Johann massaged his shoulders.

The Americans mingled easily, and Johann saw the movement of Z's forearm along the edge of the table, his hand hidden. Z sat next to Adam.

The latecomers were the Misters: Mr. Themba and Mr. Porter. Mr. Themba liked to tell jokes. "Do you know what you get when?" he said and burst out in raucous laughter. Mr. Porter just smiled and held his hand.

"Where are everyone's costumes?" Mr. Themba said thunderously when he came out onto the patio. "I thought this was a fancy dinner party. Only the very glamorous attire."

"Or the very gaudy," Mr. Porter said under his breath, with the subtle pinched smile of reserved Oxford men.

Johann slapped his hands on the table. "Precisely. It's time that I tackle the menu, and the rest of you doll up. We'll eat in one hour."

They all knew that in African time this translated into two, so no one—besides Johann—made any motion to move. Even the Americans sat awhile longer. Adam dealt another hand of euchre (which he had spent the last twenty minutes trying to teach them).

Heather slipped into the kitchen where Johann was getting a rack of lamb out of the refrigerator. He nodded towards the spice rack. "You want to help me mix some things up?"

"Sure." She took down rosemary, basil and black pepper, and they rubbed the spices onto the maroon flesh. "Thanks, Johann, for inviting me."

"You having a nice time?"

"The house is beautiful, and yes, I am having a nice time."

Johann was not. He was an ugly man with a double chin, narrow shoulders and a large belly that hung over his Boer shorts (the too-too-short khaki shorts of

Afrikaner men, their hairy legs sticking out from underneath the cutoffs, blasted tan from the intense sun). His head was shaved and his skin pockmarked. It was hard seeing him with gorgeous Z.

"You making some new friends out there tonight?" he said with a grin as he squeezed lemon over the lamb and put it into the oven.

"Yes." Though she sounded unsure.

"I'm glad you came," Johann told her.

What was the dinner party in celebration of? Johann told them each to come with their own personal, invented celebration or just to celebrate celebrations since there weren't enough of them, or rather, so many of them that they had lost any meaning whatsoever.

Johann beckoned Heather into the master bedroom, an L-shaped monstrosity that peeled open onto a sitting room and a bathroom. His bed was on a dais, and there were shelves of CDs and books and sculptures. He had an assortment of crystals on a nightstand, because he dabbled in that sort of thing, and selected a thin, purple crystal no bigger than his pinky.

"Here you go. I always like to give new friends a token, and this is a South African crystal from near where I used to live."

Heather took it with a smile. "Thanks, Johann."

He was forty years old and lonely. Maybe that's why he assembled all of these people together, to entertain in a house that wasn't his own. He reminded himself that he had been lonely as a married man too.

The kitchen began to fill with the smells of ginger and ambrosia and seared meat, and the card players were getting restless. Z undid his shirt and threw it onto Adam's legs. "I think it's time to get undressed."

In the master bedroom Z went to change, and Johann came in to get his vibrant orange suit coat and to pat Z on the butt. "Looking good." They embraced in front of the full-length mirror.

Johann sat to the left of the head of the table. He had put together a beautiful meal, and he knew it. He liked to watch Z eat, because he lifted each morsel delicately to his mouth, because he had never gotten food like this before. Johann cooked to show Z that he loved him.

He asked them to all dress up in costume. Heather blazed in the center, and Johann couldn't stop staring. In the scope of the evening, with the drought a faint cry in the background and the talk of election troubles hushed in the hills, Johann could playact that there were no problems. He wore a black costume to work, but here he would wear a different costume. For weren't they all masquerading the different parts of themselves?

When he told his wife he couldn't love her, because he loved men, the sinking of her chin was the most shocking reaction of all. Her face fell, and it was then that Johann realized that her assumption of his love was the only thing that had kept it up.

After the dishes had been stacked in the dishwasher and the guests drunk and tucked in bed, Johann slipped into his room. Z was already waiting for him, naked on top of the sheets. He didn't try to think about his own son—only four years younger than Z. He forgot about how his wife felt when he slid beside her in bed and kissed her. Z was almost frantic in his kisses, tender in his hugs. They had never made love before; other things they had done plenty of. He spooned into Z. "I saw you touch Adam."

"So? Friendly touch."

"Americans leave. Don't trust them to stick around. And the young ones kiss everyone."

"Kiss me, Johann." He kissed Z.

MR. THEMBA

Mr. Themba came in wearing a top hat and a white suit. His boyfriend, Mr. Porter, also wore white, and it made his shockingly snowy hair look dull. Mr. Themba's skin was a fine shade of coffee beans, and when he clasped Mr. Porter's hand, it looked like the perfect union of night and day. Mr. Themba also carried a walking stick, and he would hit it against each person's chair as a greeting.

"Johann," he said in his brilliant baritone. "The house looks charming, and you've arranged for us a fine group of guests." Mr. Themba had only just met the Americans, and he was particularly struck by Heather. She beamed at him from across the table then poured him a glass of champagne.

"You're the first person I've met whom I could call dignified," she told him.

He tapped his stick in time to his laughter.

They sat by the pool, playing cards. Johann didn't own the house, but he treated it like his own with the dinner parties he threw and the little explanation for how a modest hotel manager could afford such luxury. Even if it was only in Maseru, a pathetic excuse for a capital city.

Mr. Themba and Mr. Porter were already dressed for the dinner party. The others lounged in their day clothes, some wrapped in towels after a quick skinny dip in the pool.

Mr. Themba was an eccentric, but he pulled the role off splendidly. Because he and Mr. Porter owned a car, there was no need for him to traipse through the streets. He had invented his own world of flamboyant clothes, specialty wines and European music, and Mr. Porter indulged him.

When the others went to dress, the Misters went to set the dining table, Mr. Themba talking to Mr. Porter about today's headlines. This was a typical scene for how they were at home. And their home masqueraded as a clothing shop, so no one knew that they were partners of a different sort.

Mr. Themba had reinvented his life and didn't try to grapple with his past. (Though sometimes–mostly when he listened to local radio or visited his mother and ate her bread–did he completely dwell on his childhood. When he was beaten up or sodomized by a man at initiation school. He could still feel the tough, wrinkled skin of that man's hands around his neck as he held him from behind. Or trying on his older sister's rouge because he thought the whole world would look more beautiful with red cheeks.) But these memories were scattered in the clutter of his sporadic mind, and he only came across them accidentally.

He asked for more candles at dinner, not fewer, so that the eight faces looked startling as they sat down to dinner. He applauded Heather. "A rare thing of heterosexual beauty sits among us tonight."

The party laughed, and Heather's cheeks reddened in the way Mr. Themba loved. Red cheeks meant virility, passion, love, secrets. "A toast!" he declared, and though this was Johann's party, Mr. Themba sat at the head of the table.

They raised their glasses. "We have come to have a celebration of celebrations, and tonight I raise my glass in honor of you," he said, tilting his glass at Heather, "for your acceptance of our wildly sexual ambiguous company. To the Fag Hag in Fuchsia!"

Mr. Themba, more than he loved hearing his own

voice, loved hearing people laugh in response to his voice.

Mr. Themba and Mr. Porter left early. They had a drive ahead of them. Throughout the romance of the evening they were practical enough to realize that nights weren't safe for driving.

They took their leave, but not before Mr. Themba clasped Heather's hand and said, "Keep your beauty. That is a command, my darling."

She smiled and squeezed his hand. "I don't normally take orders, but I'll make an exception."

He roared. "Marvelous. Absolutely marvelous." He tipped his hat at the rest of the party–drunk with champagne and sexual tension. "Cheerio."

ADAM

Z is good-looking, but that's not reason enough for me to sleep with him.

I met Johann first, and then I met Z. At the club (which is a dirty place for us to hang out in, but left alone by the police and the Christians, so we make do). And then I met them both together and really tried not to fucking think about the night I danced with Z.

I tried to teach him to play euchre, though I knew he didn't give a flying fuck and he kept touching my leg. I might honestly think that humans are not meant to be monogamous, not when we're so charged every time someone flirts with us, touches us, licks their lips at us.

Heather said that she hates it when men gawk at her or touch her hair (and it's a great auburn color, yet she pulls it back way too much). But I get a high on it. Even perversely, it's nice to be wanted.

"Adam and I will be partners," said Z when I explained euchre was a partner game. I knew Johann watched us from the kitchen.

I'd known Cici and Heather for over two years. And within the first two months of meeting, we were tight. I stripped in front of them; we all appreciate skin–beautiful, multi-colored, sun soaked skin. Heather was the least concerned of us all, even though she must have figured out by now that Cici had a thing for her. But really, what people don't realize is that not every person who likes you is going to jump you–and not any more so because he or she is gay. So why worry about it? Heather was comfortable with her nakedness, and I loved her for it.

I'd decided to wear a blue suit and a lime-green tie. I shaped my hair into a stiff mohawk (which Heather cut for me last week) and I put Vaseline on my lips and eyelids so they shone.

We talked about love.

"It's going to happen to me eventually," Cici said, because she had recently broken up with this Mosotho radio host who I always thought was a jealous bitch and had no use for her.

"Of course it will," Heather said, soothing Cici by massaging her shoulders, and Cici grinned with not-quite-love but this sort of infatuation that she had with Heather because she couldn't have her.

Z made eyes at me over the soup. I've kissed many men. Heather already said she couldn't understand why Z would be with someone like Johann. It's not a looks thing (though that's part of it) and not an age thing (hell, Heather's pining after this thirty-eight year old Indian man) but more that they're just so wrong for each other. In my opinion, Johann showed Z how he was, and now Z needs someone who can show him how it can be.

The Misters are a perfect example of what it can be like. Mr. Themba–what a fine fairy. I swore to turn out like him when I'm fifty. He asked us all to go around and declare our celebrations. Mr. Themba said he wanted to celebrate the Fag Hag in Fuchsia. If more people were like her, we wouldn't have to cloister behind garden parties, he said. He had taken a liking to her.

When it was my turn, I said I'm celebrating new adventures though I didn't look at Z. Make what you will of adventures.

I slept next to Belinda that night. I held her and she cried, "Cici doesn't like me. There's no one for me in this place. She's a right bitch." She told me she had watched Cici's nipples all night as they poked through her gown,

23

and when she smoked the hookah she had imagined sucking on them. "I'm so goddamned pathetic."

"Hush," I said, "Just hush, baby." She smelled of ginger and apple blossoms, and I love how women smell. Men smell husky or athletic, but not women. People peg fags as always hanging on women, to soak up their femininity or something, but the real reason is their smell.

So I held Belinda and she fell asleep, quietly snoring. I was too drunk to sleep, and I thought about what I had said to Heather that night. I would be with her for the rest of my life if neither of us could find a man. It would only be the sex we wouldn't have—and ok, that's a fucking important thing—but all the other stuff: the love, the hugs, the smell, the conversations, the fights, the comfortable silences; that's a hell of a lot of stuff. I could settle for that.

I dreamt that night of Heather, and in my dreams her hair was fuchsia.

Z

He wanted me. I know. I didn't really listen as he explained the game. That queen duo Themba and Porter came in. Stupid men. Like they were a fine married couple. What a joke. Look at my *'me* and *ntate*. Married and *ntate* left and there's my *'me* saying prayers to him, and he not dead or nothing.

I ignored the men who clean the pool, even though I watched them do it this morning. They're Basotho, like me, but not like me. I got nice clothes. I got a boyfriend. I think about telling them that and seeing the looks on their faces, but Johann said I gotta be careful. Like they police or something.

This house is mega-big, like a hotel or something. (The first time I went to Johann's hotel to eat, I didn't know what to do or where to sit or what to order. First time I had ever had a cappuccino and I was…what's the word?…wired. Like a hot electric wire or something.) My 'me's house, could fit two of them inside Johann's bedroom. Our bedroom. Our bedroom, he told me to call it.

I like good food. None of this salty, tasteless shit that my 'me has been feeding me all my life. I starved today in order to eat all of Johann's food.

There was this one chick–Heather–who is straight. She sat on my lap in the car cuz there wasn't much room and she has real pretty hair, red-colored or something, and I never had met her before. But there she was sitting on my lap and everything, and Adam said she knew about us, but I didn't want her to get the wrong idea or nothing, that because I'm a man and she sat on my lap that I like her or nothing. I don't. Could forget about her. But she's, like, bright and beautiful and laughed a lot, even at Mr. Themba's jokes, and the old man is not funny or nothing.

I dipped myself in the pool, wet and long and delicious I'm like. They were all too shy to swim with me, so they watched me float, and the underwater lights made my skin sparkle like stars or something, bright on my naked black skin.

Johann told me, "Get out of that pool and get dressed." So I chose white pants and put on a fine fluffy boa around my neck for the party. Tonight that's all I planned to wear with Johann. He's got a son about my age, and I liked to tell Johann that, though he might push me away, and I liked to think that Johann's son would be the better lover—kind of shy and muscular (not like old, worn-out stretched muscles, but young and fine) and so I imagined his son's face (there's a picture by the bed) and it didn't quite feel so bad.

The food smelled so damn good, of loving oysters and fat grease, boozing champagne and medicine-powerful garlic. The food spun magic spells in our nostrils.

I never saw a white girl look so hot, like her head on fire with that hair. And she blazing in a dress out of a candy store. Shiny wrapper of aluminum and sickly neon colors that they only make in packages. I thought that color would look good on Adam, and then I'd peel it away like a chocolate bar (white chocolate ha-ha) and lick down his chest, right down his breastbone.

Some might think (like that Heather girl who shone in the candlelight and moved a candle closer to her face during dinner cuz she wanted us all to see her lips better, her throat so white with light it hurt but I couldn't look away) that a man such as my fuck-handsome-self liked every man I bumped into. But this was no truth. I didn't like Themba, and Porter I could forget about, and even some young men like BoBo, the taxi driver I met at the club. That bastard had teeth that overlapped, and he didn't ever say anything, and that silence freaked me out. He one man I didn't want.

After dinner, Belinda brought the hookah and they sat around and smoked, and I didn't smoke nothing but held Adam's hand. Adam got up to take a piss, and Heather came over, her dress so long she draped it over her arm. She sat on my lap again, uninvited, but she smelled good enough that I kept her there.

"You're too bright to look at, girl."

She laughed. "I won't stay long." She jabbed a finger at my chest. "Don't hurt Adam, okay?"

"You his guard?"

"You could say that." Sounding serious. "Don't hurt him. He likes you too much."

And that's when I knew I liked that girl.

I celebrated sex tonight. That what got me here, that what keep me going. Going on. And tonight, for the first and only time, I gave it to Johann, and I felt nothing like it before. He'd stroke my head, my chest and told me how great I could have it. How he'd send me to school, and we'd run the hotel together.

For nineteen years, no one had loved me, but Johann cared.

I once stole the sheets from Johann's guest bed cuz they so fine and soft, and I wanted that feel on my butt-naked body for always.

BELINDA

It was Belinda's idea to float paper boats in the pool. Before Mr. Themba asked for their celebrations, she proposed her own. Celebration of love and water, paper and floating. So she folded paper boats–something she learned to do in an origami class she took in England. Because there, she told Mr. Themba, they took classes for fun.

So she folded a boat for each of them and glanced out of the corners of her eyes, Heather watching her fold. Heather didn't play cards and when she drank, she said, she needed something to do. So she watched the folding of paper boats.

When the boats had been folded, Belinda handed them each a piece of paper. Write love notes, she told them, to someone you really love. But no names, she wagged a finger at them. Mr. Themba and Mr. Porter had arrived and weren't interested in the card game. Before Johann snuck off to make food, Belinda had him write a note.

Then they each tucked their note into a boat, between the paper sails. Stand by the edge of the pool, Belinda commanded. They crouched by its sparkling clear edge and let them go adrift. "Walk blindly in circles. Don't peek at the boats."

There was enough of a breeze to make this work. They walked in circles and when Belinda told them to stop, they crouched again and waited for a boat to come their way. They all drifted towards Cici, and so the others moved near her, and they each gathered a boat.

"Read your private love note."

They giggled and blushed as they read. "Man," Adam said, "I got my own note."

"Don't crumple them now," Belinda said, "but keep them until this evening. When the second part of the celebration will commence."

Belinda opened hers. It read: You are beautiful. Ravishing. I love more than just your skin, your sweetness, your soft curves. I love your laughter and your frown, and it gives me heartache that I cause neither. Love you baby girl.

Belinda knew it was Cici's note. And knew it wasn't for her.

She sat by Porter and Heather at dinner, and couldn't stand to look at Heather, whom Cici paid attention to.

She focused on her food and Mr. Porter's mumblings, for he wouldn't loudly respond to any question or comment but would mumble his responses, and so it felt like a private conversation between him and her.

Belinda hadn't been back long, but simultaneously both England and home felt oceans away. There was distance here now, and she couldn't patch it or lessen it. She didn't feel English in the way Mr. Porter looked English, and she was no longer black the way Z was (and she had known Z as a child and knowing him as a man made her feel old and used up). Belinda used to sing jingles on the radio and could speak four languages. This made her marketable. She also posed in an ad for a billboard for the phone company Vodacom. The company had painted her teeth white and told her to suck in her belly. That had been a long time ago.

No one recognized her voice now. Everyone oversaw her looks. She hid her looks behind a mask tonight. The ticklish peacock-blue feathers framing her eyes and mouth. And here she sat by a strangely pretty white woman who wasn't in love with any of them and yet who created a stream of love around the table.

The second part of Belinda's celebration began at the hookah. She brought it to smoke, and they sat in the music room on cushions (though no one, not even the well-bred Mr. Porter, could play the baby grand), their costumes rumpled. Belinda's mask sat atop her head, and she asked to see the notes. They pulled them forth from pockets and breasts and read them aloud.

Then they torched them in the hot coals of the fireplace and watched the love notes burn.

Belinda cried that night in Adam's arms, but didn't tell him that she had kept Cici's love note and burned a plain piece of paper in its place.

MR. PORTER

I let my dear Mr. Themba do the talking. I loved the man, but he talked far too much. I invented symphonies in my head when I didn't feel like listening. I missed playing the French horn, which was what I did before winding up in Africa. But that was the first of several lifetimes, and dwelling on it only made me feel–empty? Sad? Tired?

I thought the suit was costume enough. I wasn't disappointed about how I was to spend my evening, but I preferred to experience it in my own way.

Mr. Themba said we were our own "wives club" and it's hideous, and rather pathetic, how we don women's titles when there are no male titles fitting for us. Wives, queens, fairies, bitches. I liked to think of us as the Misters Club. Two old gentlemen in our suspenders and boxers, making tea after shop hours, listening to Tchaikovsky or Handel.

I left England and never found my way home, but that was one reason why I loved to visit Johann. Tonight it was the Dutch ambassador's and the scent of Europe hung heavy in the air. It cloaked the patio and the dining room and the sleek modern bathroom where I went to splash water on my face.

I bumped into the nice young lady, Heather, when I came out of the bathroom. She was oddly pleasing,

31

reminded me greatly of my niece (from an Irish mother) who lived in London. Hadn't seen her in over twelve years. She would look similar to Heather, who laughed more than Helen ever did.

"Sometimes you have to escape, you know?" Heather spoke as she stepped into the loo to wash her hands. "Too many people can crowd the mind."

I handed her a towel. "I couldn't have put it better myself."

I wandered through the rooms, flipped through the art books on the coffee table in the living room—proof of culture in this household, read a selection of Milton in the music room, sniffed the daisies on the dining table, and draped myself across the chaise lounge. I lay there when the young Americans strolled by, going to the opposite wing to dress for dinner. Heather wagged her fingers at me.

How had we all ended up here? And had anyone thought about where we were headed after this evening? The two young ones—Adam and Z—didn't know what they were getting into. They didn't know that Love and Lust are border towns.

At dinner, Heather was the last to arrive. We loved beauty, re-created it at our parties, in our clothing, in the way we spoke. I kept satin to my ties, but she wore so much in a way I have yet to do for myself. We liked her because she was beautiful, but non-threatening. Her beauty to be admired not envied, and we liked to be surrounded by beauty. We were, simply, aesthetes.

Heather sat where I couldn't see her, but her laugh rang down the table when Mr. Themba said, "The Fag Hag in Fuchsia!"

She reminded me of the first person I loved, and believe it or not, I did once love a woman. A girl, I suppose. Her name was Eleanor, and she played the trumpet. An unfeminine instrument for a girl so delicate and red-haired. She would puff her cheeks out at me over pints after rehearsals to make me laugh, but it succeeded in making her laugh. Heather's laughs reminded me of Eleanor.

And then the satin. Eleanor always wore a black satin gown to concerts. She was wearing that gown when I told her I couldn't love her anymore.

"My lovely Mr. Porter," Mr. Themba said and pulled on my shirtsleeve, "let's start with you." He raised his glass. "What do you celebrate this evening?"

The faces around the table blurred behind the candle flames. The stems of glasses hovered between their fingers in ready anticipation.

"I celebrate the music of laughter."

Heather was the first to break the clink of the cheers. She laughed.

Mr. Themba and I were the first to leave that night. I held Mr. Themba's arm, his white suit coat in his free hand.

"I love you, Edmund," he said to me and kissed my

cheek.

"Come along," I told him. "Leave those words for home."

CICI

Cici liked her women exotic, voluptuous and feisty. She had been seeing Ruby, this local chick that worked at Johann's hotel. She had been seeing Ruby, but was in love with Heather. Mostly because she couldn't have her. Heather was a mystery. She smiled at Cici and Cici burned.

Cici had spent a number of nights at Johann's. She worked right outside of the capital, and came in every weekend to dance, buy groceries and see Ruby. She lived a dual life.

Cici was the one who told Heather about Johann–the one who had pushed Heather to find the beautiful gown to wear as her costume–the one who had whispered, "don't worry, you'll have a great time" in Heather's ear when she sat on Z's lap in the car because the others were essentially strangers to Heather.

Cici wasn't sure if what she had with Johann was a friendship or not. He cooked her food, and she talked, and they danced in the club, but she never told him things–not secrets or memories or daydreams or ramblings. Cici could tell Heather these things.

Cici watched Heather get up to help Johann in the

kitchen. "Ooh-ooh," Adam said close to the curve of her neck.

"What?"

"I saw your eyes."

Cici grinned. "Yeah, there are always wishes."

He patted her head and then lay down a card. "Don't undervalue a friend, Cici."

"Stick to your card game, Adam."

Cici knew Belinda got her love note, and she also knew that Belinda had feelings for her (but what did that mean? To have feelings like having a mortgage, a burden, a baby?). Mostly she knew because Belinda didn't seem to like Heather. Adam loved Heather–told her he'd marry her if the two of them wound up single. Johann took to her quickly. And Z even flirted with her in his youthful, charming way. Mr. Themba and she talked clothing, and Mr. Porter and she talked literature.

Belinda avoided her.

And avoided Cici when they all went to get dressed that evening. Cici wore a stretchy black dress with silver Dorothy glitter shoes and a scarf wrapped up in her hair. She had large breasts like sandbags, and she didn't wear a bra, so her nipples stuck out raw and button-like beneath her dress. She loved her curves and would hug herself as she lay in bed on the bare nights when Ruby wasn't there.

She helped Heather zip up the dress. "The Dress" as it came to be known after that night. It was scandalous and fabulous all at once—something a bit unheard of here. It dipped low in back and draped across her breasts. It was sleeveless, and the thin straps that held it up had jewels sewn into them. The fabric wound around her waist, showing off her waist, and then fell in waves from her hips, falling in layers of vibrant fuchsia silk.

Oh? What did Cici celebrate that night? The delicacy of the appetite.

When Heather fell asleep against Cici's shoulder, she tried not to move and to soak up the heat that Heather's body emitted. When it got to be too much, she almost got up. She even had thoughts of kissing Belinda, who got up at around the same time and went to the bathroom that joined their twin rooms. She peed with the doors cracked open, and Cici liked that familiarity. Like they were all part of one rainbow-colored fucked-up family.

And like Heather and Belinda were her sisters. And you didn't kiss your sisters.

She made cinnamon pancakes in the morning. She watched Heather add tablespoons of margarine and very lightly dampen her cakes with golden syrup. She couldn't eat, and so she watched the others. Johann came out late, and sat down cautiously on a stool, looking sheepish as his eyes met Cici's. Belinda tore at her pancakes with her fingers and swirled them around in a puddle of syrup, but didn't eat. Adam went to pack and Z went to wash up in the guest bathroom, but neither came back for quite sometime.

Cici watched the shape of Heather's mouth as she ate pancakes. Watching people eat usually made her want to puke, but Heather guarded her mouth with her hand as she chewed, so Cici only saw the ripple of her mouth corners and the bob of her jaw, and she could almost be glad that it was her food in Heather's mouth.

HEATHER

I had a love affair with the world. I had never met the non-Americans before, besides Johann, and him only at the hotel where he worked and served us volunteers drinks. I put away the cruelties of the clinic I worked at, the drama of the Indian man I had fallen in love with, and concentrated on having a party. The smell of chlorine was a great relief, like remembering the other world I once existed in. Has it really been two years now? Years that wiped out what came before. I signed on for a third year because as much as I wanted to go back–scribbled daydreams down in my journal–I wouldn't be the same person if I returned, and this new version of me wouldn't fit. So I stayed.

It hadn't always been good to me, but don't we sometimes love those that abuse us? And it became difficult working in the clinic, where I'm asked for money I don't have, and marriage proposals I would never accept (because can we love those that we don't know?) Someone, please define love for me.

Love might be this party. To share food and music with once-strangers and eggshell friends. Friendships that are robin-blue with newness and fragility.

I've seen shades of blue today: the blue vinyl of Johann's car as I gripped his headrest while I tried not to put all of my weight on Z's lap. Light as a feather, stiff as a board. God, those childhood games seem distant, like someone else's lifetime I am remembering. They don't play games like those in places like these. The blue of the guard's shirt as he let us into the drive—there's a barbed gate a determined person couldn't scale. The blue of the pool water (and how does it get that aquamarine blue? The chemicals? The reaction with the sun?) The blue of Z's skin, because it has that sheen of tar. The blue of Cici's eyes, because I knew she watched me. The blue of the dinner plates, Mr. Themba's scarf, the label of the beer, the gleam in the crystal, the dotted pattern in the pillowcase as my face lay near Cici's.

But this was far from a night of feeling blue. This was a night of celebrations.

We played cards to distract us enough until we were drunk. So we could meet each other and not blush when we looked at one another, and everyone else thought about who they would kiss if they could.

I knew Belinda didn't like me, and I didn't push conversation. I loved her ideas of love notes though. I had these secret dreams to be a poet. Though it was neither practiced nor published. I deliberated a bit longer over my poem than necessary. I'm sure Adam thought I was writing to the Indian guy I had been seeing (though it's such an American concept to "see" someone and this might be why it wasn't working).

Instead, because I couldn't think of anything to say, I wrote down this snippet, from Auden: "To settle in this village of the heart. My darling, can you bear it?"

I didn't want to be awkward. I never thought it made sense to feel isolated or to group yourself by the person you'd most want to sleep with. And that's funny because I've never slept with the Indian, and I am a declared virgin in all this mix.

Mr. Themba and Mr. Porter remind me of grandfathers. "Wouldn't it be great," I said into Adam's ear, practically kissing his earlobe, "if when we get older we pair off with a best friend–maybe a lover–but that everyone was in pairs of grandfathers and grandmothers. We'd be less bitter that way."

Adam stroked his ear where I imagined my breath had tickled him. "I'd be yours forever, Heather."

If only I could box up his words and put it under a Christmas tree (which doesn't exist here). I'd open it when I became wrinkled and under loved.

I followed Johann into the kitchen. Z rubbed Adam's thigh, and I wasn't prepared to be witness to that.

The scent of cooking reminded me of my father, who

made Sunday breakfasts while my mom lounged in her robe with a good mystery novel in front of the mute TV. I placed my hands on the steel sink, the slick countertops, the cool refrigerator that hummed with electricity, tapped my knuckles on the rack of pans that hung over the island and told Johann, "I love the smell of spices." From the kitchen I could watch the others.

"I'm nervous about tonight," Johann said.

"The party will be fun."

He smiled slyly.

"Ah, you don't mean the party."

I brought Johann the extra love note that was meant for him, because he was still cooking. "What does this mean?" he asked. "Village of the heart?"

I smiled. "It's just poetry, I suppose." Then I went to dress.

There weren't any vivid memories left in my head about dressing up. I once attended prom and wedding dances and even hit up clubs, but now I worked. And The Dress felt like magic, better than the hot shower I took the minute I arrived. Spiking hot water that stripped my skin of the dust, filthy heat and germs.

Cici zipped it up for me. And her fingers scratched my back, right between the shoulder blades, where, when I stretch my chest and pull my elbows closer together, the blades stick out like broken birds' wings, bony and dead of flight. And sometimes I felt like a clipped bird, stranded in Lesotho. (This is bird-watching country, though never had I spotted an ornithologist stuck to her binoculars, mimicking the cries of the mokhotlo bird.)

Birds were on my mind at dinner, when Johann carved the chicken and the skin was crispy. I ate both wings in its honor.

The moon had been plucked, picked apart, placed in the candles, and everyone looked beautiful. If I could capture this scene: the steaming food rich in color, the odd assortment of costume–silk and bright hues and flouncy feathers–the grins and jokes and anticipation raining down as we prepared our celebrations–then there wouldn't be so much fear of them. They'd–in their oddities–look normal to the rest of the world. Like a family at Thanksgiving. Of course, there aren't any Thanksgivings here.

Mr. Themba slightly scared me, merely because he isn't scared of anything. He looked at the space between my breasts, but what was he searching for? I placed a hand over my heart and laughed.

"Darling Fag Hag, what do you celebrate?"

Yes, the outsider. Labeled in my own way, though they wouldn't think of it like that. "Uncaged birds." Mr. Themba whistled, and I laughed.

Later on in the evening, Z cawed and flapped his arms, completely drunk as he spun about the music room. "I am your bird," he told me and kissed me on the cheek. Maybe in the light he mistook me for Adam. Soon after he darted into Johann's bedroom and stayed there for the night. I knew Adam wanted him to come out, and I wrapped my arms around Adam's waist and kissed his back. It was so much easier to love those you will never have.

The night fizzled out, and after the Misters got into the car, we smoked the hookah awhile longer, inhaling mango and peach, puffing out slow-telling stories about people we had loved, daring feats we had done, dreams we once had. And only in the smoke could we say them clearly. Everyone's eyes got blurry, and our shoulders slumped in the comfort of being high. And we weren't so rigid, and I let my knee bump Cici's, and rest there.

My dress napped across the foot of our bed, Cici's body heat strangely comforting, and in the morning I'd get to leave, still the same, my love open even beyond this gated house.

"Do you love him?" Cici meant the guy I was dating.

"I don't love him any more than I've loved anyone else."

"Tell me a story." So I told her a fairy tale, because that's all I could think of.

"There's no happily ever after," I warned.

She nestled into my shoulder. "I don't believe in those anyway."

When I heard Cici breathing heavily and Belinda's whimpering die down in the adjoining room, I got up.

Draping the dress around my shoulders, which was surprisingly warm, I wandered the rooms. Smoke and alcohol made it difficult for me to sleep. The fire wasn't quite out in the music room, and in the ashes where we burnt the notes, someone had traced the word LOVE, the V barely visible, so it could've read: LONE, LOSE, LORE.

I walked around the pool, and there were cigarette butts and beer bottles, and a single feather floated on top of the water's surface. I touched the water with my toes, and it was frigid. In the kitchen I drank a glass of milk, refreshing compared to the powdered milk I was so used to, and plucked a grape from the fruit bowl. It burst in my mouth.

Staying away from Johann's room, where the soft guttural groans of pleasure eked out slowly, I wove back through the rooms. Lingering in the dining room, I sat at the head of the table, crumbs decorating the tablecloth. I sat amidst the dying candle stubs and scattered chairs, the smells of wine and spices in the air.

Shades of White

The baby sucks on sugar cubes. She has a tooth coming in and gritty sweetness feels good on her gums. Ana doesn't know about the sugar, but she leaves baby Clara in the hands of Q. And if it stops her crying, then Q thinks it's ok. Also, if Clara doesn't finish the cube, then Q takes the last bit and puts it on her own tongue and the shock of raw sugar makes her feel good.

"Q, take the baby inside," Ana told her. Ana meant inside the bungalow, not the hostel that she and her boyfriend Jan own next door. So Q took the baby inside and fed her sugar.

Q isn't her real name. Her real name is Qenehelo, but in Sesotho the Q is a click and Ana didn't want to pronounce it, so she asked Q for her Christian name when she hired her (because all Basotho have Christian names) but funny enough, Q's name was also Anna–though with two Ns–and Ana had said, "That won't do." And so she decided to call her Q.

Q doesn't argue, because it doesn't matter what you are called as long as you are paid.

Q sometimes wishes that she had a camera and could take a photograph, like the photos Jan takes for the hostel brochures–of golden walls and viny gardens and a pool that's bright like the underbelly of a seashell. Then she would have a photo taken of her and the baby Clara, sitting just like this on the rag carpet, with sugar in their mouths.Clara sitting in white ruffles and Q in her maid's uniform of blue polyester, the sun through the French doors shining equally on Clara's pink skin and Q's brown skin.

She would like a photo of herself on the beach too, barefoot in the white-peaked waves. But only tourists take photos like that, and even though the ocean is just over the building tops—a seagull's flight away—Q never has time to enjoy it. She went there once with Ana and Clara. Ana bought an ice cream cone and refused to walk on the sand because Clara would get dirty. She ate the cone and Q held the baby and they watched the waves, but didn't touch them. So Q knows only the look of waves.

Q never asks herself why she came to Portsmeade. South Africa has jobs—more jobs than Q's native land of Lesotho—and all of her brothers and cousins and friends who crossed the border never came back. She knew then it had to be better.

There aren't many white people in Lesotho, and Q only knows the Irish priest who is very red in the face and speaks Sesotho and works at the local church. He has never personally talked to Q, so she doesn't know what to make of him. Ana is more her idea of a white person, strangely beautiful and thin with hair that spills down her back. And if it feels anything like Clara's wisps of hair, it is fine and soft like sifted flour.

Jan, ugly and broad-shouldered, frightens Q. She disappears when he comes into the room—demanding a cold drink or a clean shirt or complaining to Ana that Tumelo, the gardener, is not doing his job properly. Q moves slowly and doesn't breathe and her eyes look anywhere but at Jan.

Unless, of course, she's spoken to. Then she inclines her head in Jan's direction and keeps her eyes focused on his chest. In the hot African noons, he unbuttons his shirt, and she sees the twisted brown hairs plastered to his sweaty chest. Q thinks a white person should be white all over.

When Clara finishes the sugar cube, she smacks her lips and drifts into a delicate nap. Q gets up and folds the hostel sheets. Corner to corner, snapped taut, end to end, and folded over. Then folded again and smoothed into a nice, perfect white rectangle. White sheets look crisp and pure and expensive, Ana has told her, but they're harder to keep clean. So Q spends many of her days washing and drying and folding cloud-white sheets.

When the sheets are folded and stacked, Q gently picks up Clara who murmurs baby nonsense, and hoists her onto her back. She drapes a blanket around Clara and ties it in front, across her chest. She tucks it securely in back under the baby's bottom, pinning it with a long silver pin. This is how Basotho women carry their babies, and the baby feels the warmth of the mother's back and can smell the soap of her skin and feel safe. Q gets more work done this way.

She goes next door to the hostel, making sure to lock the sunroom door. Q carries a set of keys, hidden in her bosom, and whenever she leaves or enters the home or the gates—even for a second—she must lock the doors. Ana and Jan don't trust people, not the tourists and certainly not the people outside of the gated walls. She goes out the front gate, walks down the street. The sheets are in her arms, her chin resting on them.

The wall of Ana's property is made of cement, painted blue and gold. The sunlight plays on the top of the wall, slapping the shards of glass that are imbedded there, stuck up in jagged peaks to deter intruders. But in the sun they are brilliant, and red, green and silver light races across the wall top.

The gate to the hostel is open. It is near Easter, and tourists from Japan and America and Australia have been arriving daily, in loud, camera-clicking groups—pale and suntanned and slender. They carry backpacks, their legs a shock of skin thrusting out from short shorts. Q always feels embarrassed and slightly in awe as she turns her head away at the sight of them.

Q has to wear a uniform. The skirt is long and the shoulders of the dress come down to her pointed elbows. She is small, with a round head and a flat nose. Her shoulders are small too and her arms are muscular, her chest flat. She has no waist, but her hips are wide, and her butt scoops outward like a clay bowl. She never shows her legs.

Q takes the sheets into the linen room, which houses a wash sink and cupboards for all the hostel linen. There is a cot there too, on those rare nights when Ana makes her stay while she and Jan go out. The whole room is done up in shades of white: sugar-white, eyeball-white, milk-white, Ana's skin-white. Q decides that God must not have been able to decide on one white, so he gave the world a hundred different shades, and they are all in Ana's linen room.

She comes out of the linen room and Ana is helping two young men with their luggage. Ana smiles and laughs with them. When she sees Q she automatically orders, "Q, get me key number seven."

Q ignores the boys, who joke about their experience in a South African taxi, and moves past Ana and into the reception. She takes key number seven off its hook behind the desk and brings it back to Ana. Clara awakens and Q hears her gurgle, and a small pink fist knocks Q's shoulder as Clara reaches for her mother.

Ana ignores the small hand. "Let me show you room seven," she tells the boys, taking a duffle bag in each hand. "Q, get two beers from the icebox and have them ready at the bar."

Jan is in the kitchen, which is right off of the bar. He is fixing egg and cheese toasties for two other guests. He stands at the stove, barefoot, wearing green board shorts and a shirt that Q ironed that morning. He smells of fresh laundry–sun dried and soaped–and cooking grease.

Q opens the beers and keeps the tops in her pocket. She knows a woman in the township who makes candleholders and souvenirs out of beer caps, and Q will take them to her tonight, and in exchange she'll have fresh bread baking for Q. This is the deal they've silently made.

Jan comes up behind Q, his breath pungent like onions. Jan rubs Clara's waving fist and leans over and kisses it. "Do you like your job?" he asks Q.

"Yes."

"You could lose your job, you know? Ana thinks you're taking the baby from her."

Q wipes perspiration from the bottles.

"I can let you keep your job." He strokes her skin with the spatula that still carries heat.

Q hears laughter from outside, and Jan steps away. She rubs her arm where the spatula touched her, which is worse than Jan touching her, because Q knows he won't touch her in public. He wants to, but he won't, and that makes Q feel diseased.

Ana comes into the bar with the boys. Q thinks they must be American or Canadian; she can never quite tell the difference. She likes to listen to the sound of their voices and in the corners of rooms she mimics their "heys" and "see yas" though she never gets to use them.

The boys take their beers, and one boy nods at Q and

thanks her, so she nods then moves away into the kitchen. Jan finishes the toasties and carries them out to one of the dining tables, and comes back with Ana. Clara fusses and Q reaches back and pats her bottom, clucking under her breath.

"Why does she insist on carrying the baby like that?" Jan says to Ana. He places a hand on Clara's head.

"It's how they all carry their babies."

"A baby should be carried properly, not like some damn net of fish strung across the back. Her head will bounce around."

Ana shrugs and looks out at the bar. The Americans (Q decides they're American) are laughing, their arms draped with ease along the backs of their chairs.

Jan slams cupboard drawers, clatters about in the jar of cooking utensils and jostles the knives. "If Q had a baby she'd understand how to carry one."

"Shh," Ana says, turning to Jan. "Q has a child."

"Where?"

"In Lesotho. I think she left it with her mother."

Jan grunts. "Some mother she makes." He fishes around in the icebox for a beer, pops the top, and goes out to the bar to join his guests. They shake hands, exchange names, talk about the surf.

Ana sighs. "Q, take the baby out to the garden. Stay out of the sun though; I don't want her to get brown."

Q goes to the garden the long way, deciding not to go past the bar and out onto the patio. She goes around to

50

the side garden gate instead and welcomes the deep shade of the palm trees. Tumelo, the gardener, is keeping up appearances. Q unties Clara from her back and watches Tumelo work.

Q knows that Tumelo has seen her, but he keeps on working, disregarding her presence. A few months ago Tumelo told Q he would buy her a mobile phone or new clothes or take her to the Cape Town Fish Market in Durban for dinner, if only she would sleep with him. It's not an unusual request; many men with a bit of money offer gifts to young women, in exchange for some favor. Tumelo is not rich, but he is old and has worked for years and managed to save a little. Q was annoyed by his offer. She works. She supports herself. Tumelo seemed almost offended by her refusal, and they haven't spoken much since.

Tumelo picks up leaves. The garden surrounds the enclosed pool with grass that is maternally watered and clipped, even in drought, and with shady palms that block out the fierce sun during the hottest afternoon hours. Ana says she wants serenity and beauty and perfection out in the gardens. So Tumelo picks up all of the leaves that have fallen–on the grass, in the stone cracks of the path, on the shiny surface of the pool water.

Q asks, "What do you do with all of those leaves?"

She thinks Tumelo will ignore her. But finally he looks at her and pats his pocket. "I put them here. Then I toss them away."

Q thinks it's almost tragic. That the trees and flowers have given pieces of themselves to the ground–to Tumelo and Ana–only to get thrown away. The leaves are shed like tears are shed–uncounted and wiped away.

Tumelo stoops over and offers Q a long, pointed red leaf that fell from one of the plants. He places it in her open palm, which is like the film of creamed-coffee skated over with age lines.

"It's always good to have something beautiful to hold," he tells her and goes back to work. He blends into the garden greens as natural as dirt.

A duo of Japanese girls drifts by, in matching polka-dot swimming suits and sunglasses as big and round as melon halves, and so inky black that Q can't see their eyes. They dip their toes into the pool, and Tumelo walks around them, picking up leaves.

Q plays with Clara on the ground, tickling her with the red leaf, and Clara's giggles are throaty and warbled like birds. Q counts Clara's fingers and toes in English and Afrikaans and Sesotho, teaching Clara all of her tongues. And Q wonders to herself: how many years will it be before Clara stops seeing her? Two? Three? The paleness of Clara's eyes will fail to see Q over time until Q is nothing but a shadow–hovering on the periphery of her sight–ready to flash into slight existence when needed or spoken at.

The bar opens onto the dining room, which flows out

to the patio that overlooks the garden. From the garden patio Q sees Jan and the American boys on their second beers, hands waving and slapping as they talk.

Q gets the broom to sweep away the dust and ants from the patio. She continues into the dining room where the guests who had the toasties left crumbs. There are crumbs on the table and the benches and the floor. Q sweeps them up.

Ana had hired a Zulu girl to keep the hostel clean, but she stole money from one of the guest's rooms and that was the end of her. Q felt sorry for her because the girl was an orphan and took care of her four sisters, but then Q stopped feeling sorry for her because she had her own job to do.

Tumelo cares for the gardens. Q cares for the baby. And Clementine—a honey-faced woman of 40—cares for the hostel rooms. Jan cooks meals, because he can drink alcohol and talk to guests, and Ana makes sure that everyone does their job. Of course, Q has to keep Ana's house cleaned too, but she doesn't cook because Jan says he doesn't like Bantu food and fears poison and germs and raw meat. Q never undercooks her meat, but since she doesn't particularly enjoy cooking, she doesn't mind.

Q unwraps the baby and lets her down. Clara crawls to Jan while Q sweeps the floor, and Jan sweeps Clara into his arms.

"Why would they want to take your hostel?" Q overhears one of the boys asking Jan.

"Because," he practically shouts, bouncing Clara on his knee, "the government says this hostel is on property that rightfully belongs to *them*. Rightfully, my ass. By law I bought this place and fixed it up. And I pay the taxes. I have the right to it. I didn't take their land."

"Well, I suppose they're trying to be fair."

"Fair? Is it fair that I put all of this time and money and labor into this place, for them to take it away and let it become run down? Believe me, those people don't know how to take care of things properly."

"It seems that South Africa's done pretty well for itself, I mean since apartheid ended."

"Yeah," the other boy says, "Nelson Mandela did a good job as president, right?"

Jan tickles the baby under her chin. "Nelson Mandela? He's a terrorist. A murderer."

"Really?" one boy says, looking at his friend. "That's not what we hear back home."

"That's why more people like you need to go back to America and tell the truth about him."

The boys drink. One of the boys spots Q and nudges his friend. Quickly, they talk about soccer.

"The Kaiser Chiefs are the only team," Jan hoots, as he motions for Q to take the baby.

Q passes through the bar and out of the reception.

Ana gives Q one hundred rand for groceries. This is more than Q makes in a week, and Q works every day.

She arrives on the earliest taxi from the township where she stays, at 6 a.m., and then she stays until past dinnertime and leaves at 7 p.m. There is never time off because there's no time off for a hostel or from motherhood, Ana tells her.

It's been ten months since Q left her village in Lesotho. She saved up one hundred rand to send back to her family. In ten months, she saved up what Ana spends on one week's groceries.

Q places Clara into her playpen in the house. Ana is in the next room balancing the account book for the hostel. She does this every Monday, when she sends Q off to buy groceries at the same time.

Q walks down the sloping road to Kingston Street, a busy roadway that follows the curve of the beach. The railroad tracks and the tall sweeping trees filled with vervet monkeys obscure Q's view of the ocean. But she is almost content with the knowledge that just past those trees the waves are swelling and crashing, in and out upon the shore.

She gets the groceries at the local SPAR. She picks up bread and cheese, milk and butter, sugar, mangoes, bananas, potatoes, eggs, Cadbury chocolate, shortbread cookies, jam, tea, mincemeat and a whole chicken. When Q works, she eats whatever Clara has, and when she returns to the township she has bread, boiled maize meal and greens.

She loads the groceries into canvas bags and loops

them on her wrists and ties one to her back, and balances one on her head. It's a treacherous climb up the hill to the hostel, but Q moves slowly, carefully. In Lesotho, she used to carry buckets of water on her head, since she was five years old, so groceries are not a great challenge.

Q unlocks the house gate, which requires putting down the bags in her arms, bending deeply at the knees, but maintaining a straight spine, so the bag on her head doesn't shift. As she passes through the gate, a child of about eleven or twelve creeps along the wall with outstretched hands. "Money, mother, money."

Q has change in her pocket, but instead she says, "Get" and shuts the gate.

Q enters the bungalow through the kitchen door. She hears shouting coming from the front room.

"It's pathetic," Jan says. Clara begins to scream. "You throw yourself at them, and they're boys, fifteen years younger than you."

"You're talking crazy," Ana says in a neutral tone.

Q slowly unpacks, careful not to make herself too visible in the doorway that separates the kitchen from the front room.

"Am I? Am I?" Q imagines what Jan looks like as he says this. He is probably shaking and spitting. "He asked you for a drink."

"You drink with the guests."

"I'm being a gracious host. You're just being a slut."

"Stop it, Jan. You're upsetting the baby."

"Where's her nanny? We pay her to work."

"She's getting groceries."

"Stealing groceries is more likely."

Q fingers Ana's change. Ana might not notice if a few rand were missing. Q holds the warm coins in her hand–eight or nine rand at the most–but then sets them down on the countertop. She finishes putting away the food and stands in the doorway, making herself present.

"Q," Ana says. Not as a question or an exclamation, but merely as a statement.

Jan turns and glares. "See to the baby." Q crosses the room, picks up Clara and rubs her back. Jan ignores her. "How many men will it take for you to be satisfied?"

"That's not how it is."

"Explain it to me. You want adventure? A younger man? An American man? Next thing you'll be sleeping with a kaffir man."

"Stop it." Ana sits on the edge of the sofa, looking out the French doors. The light comes through them and illuminates Ana's profile.

"Stop it or what?"

"Stop it or I'll leave you. I'll take the baby and leave."

Jan gets in her face, hunched over, the edges of his open shirt floating down on her shoulder. "I own this house."

"And I paid for the hostel."

"Which you might be losing, in case you haven't heard."

Ana shrugs. "At least I'll have Clara."

"The baby is half mine too."

"Then you can come visit us."

Jan slaps her across the face. Ana loses her composure for a moment–her eyes widen and her mouth falls open in a small *o*. She lifts her hand to her face. He slaps her again. "You think you're something special? I can have other women." He smirks, his nostrils flaring. He stands up and begins to button his shirt. "This hostel works because of me, just remember that." He opens up the French doors but then turns to face Q. "I need you to stay the night," he says. He walks out, leaving Q to stare at Ana.

Ana tucks her knees into her chest and smooshes into the sofa cushions. Her cheeks burn red, and Q sees her lips tremble, but Ana doesn't cry. "Why does this keep happening?" she asks softly.

Q stays in the corner of the room. "I had a man who did it to me, and I did it to him. It's hard to love just one person."

"It is, but why?"

Q shakes her head. "Maybe if you give your love all to one person and they stop loving you, then you've lost it and have nothing more to give. But if you give it in pieces, you only lose pieces. Slowly."

Ana looks at Q with child-like surprise. "Yeah, that's exactly how it is."

Q raises her eyes to meet Ana's eyes. Q's black and

large, Ana's wet and blue–faded like a memory of the ocean. Clara giggles and tugs on Q's ear, gently, and nuzzles against her like a newborn lamb. Q loves the feel of Clara in her arms and against her skin, her baby breath soft and milky on her neck.

Ana blinks quickly and sits up, owning herself again. "Give me the baby."

Q hands Clara to Ana, who kisses the baby's head. Ana hugs the squirming Clara and settles into the sofa.

Q goes outdoors. The ocean is only a few minutes walk away. She never leaves the house without a purpose, but she can't stay inside it a moment longer. Her arms are light without the weight of the baby or groceries or stacks of laundry. They swing by her sides, and the breeze sweeps up and under her arms and through her fingers. She crosses Kingston Street. Then she crosses the railroad tracks and picks her way through the overgrown trees. Monkeys hoot from the canopy.

She can smell the ocean from here. It smells briny and ageless–not old, not fresh, but like it has been there forever, getting better with time. Q thinks that the ocean must have been here forever, and if she were God she would have created the world as a bowl of water and placed the lands of countries into the water like lily pads. She reaches the beach, which is a mix of blonde sand and brown dirt by the edge of the trees. She takes off her shoes and places them neatly, side by side, by the foot of a tree. She walks barefoot through the sand, getting closer to the water's edge.

It is near the end of the day and few people are on the beach. Q sees a black man selling carved animals and two white teenagers holding hands, walking in the sand. Q lifts up her skirt and walks into the water. It is cold, and the foam tickles her toes. A wave crests up to her shins and splashes the hem of her dress. She pulls the skirt up higher and walks the length of the beach, the sun at her back, the hollow sound of the water her only companion.

She knows she will go back to the hostel. She'll do her job. And those thoughts buoy in the back of her mind.

For this moment only, Q has the ocean to herself.

Call From a Manchester Flat

She called from her Manchester flat at a reasonable time. She leaned on the window sill of the one street-facing window and watched the mid-afternoon traffic. She liked that the British drove on the left side of the road. Unlike the Germans or the French, who drove on the right side. She found that confusing. This was the only similarity she found with the street below and her home. Here was her home now, she supposed, but she meant the home of her family. If there had been any more similarities she might have just become sad.

She dialed the long string of numbers to the phone in her father's shop, the only phone (that she could remember) within fifteen kilometers of the village.

"Hullo?" her father shouted, because he actually thought that his volume needed to reach England. "So good of you to call."

"Yes, how are you?" She only spoke in English, not to show off her newly minted accent and hip slang, but to let her father practice his. This is what she told herself.

"Very well, thank you. And you?"

"Oh, tolerable."

"Hmm? What's that now?"

"How is mum?"

"Oh, yes, she is sick."

"Sick?" Slight alarm in her voice, though she tried not to betray this. She took a little breath like she learned in yoga class. "Sick?"

"Yes, yes. A big cough. It shakes her body. She tries to speak but only coughs. She tries to laugh–coughs instead. She is very loud."

"Has she seen a doctor?" She saw a lady's doctor now. The first time it had scared her to have this lady's doctor (a *female* lady's doctor) look between her legs with metal forceps. Everything seemed to be made out of metal in this country.

"Well, yes, six months ago. It is very difficult to travel there."

"Perhaps. She should wear a scarf and drink lots of tea with honey."

"Honey, you say?"

"Yes." Good, now she felt like she had done something. She rapped her newly polished nails against the windowpane. She pretended to be tapping on the heads of people who walked by. *Tap* on the butcher…*tap* on the baker…*tap* on the computer maker….

"Yes, next time we go to Butha-Buthe we'll go to the Chinese shop. They have honey."

"Yes, the Chinese do have everything."

Why did she say that? Her lab partner was Chinese–a sallow-faced nice girl name Mingxia. She called her Minnie. And Minnie called her Bibi. They all had nicknames here.

"So when do you think you will go next? To Butha-Buthe?"

"Oh." Her father hummed. "Maybe two weeks. Maybe three. It is hard to guess with time."

"We don't guess time here. The British are very exact."

"Why exact? The British do not control the setting sun. Up and down. Up and down. No help from the British."

"Hmm." She listened, but this conversation was the same as so many others.

"There is a new teacher at our primary school. She has come from Ireland."

"I've been to Ireland. Very green. Very beautiful." She had liked it because it rained so much, and back home there was so little rain.

"Yes. From Ireland. She stays here. Lives in the old house."

"I'm sure it's an adventure for her." Her father didn't "get" sarcasm. But she didn't understand those people–the Irish, the British, Australians–Americans were the worst she discovered. Living in a hut was some idea of an adventure. Because it wasn't permanent, she decided. Things were manageable when they weren't permanent.

"…and her Sesotho is so funny. We laugh."

"I'm sure she loves that."

"Who does not love a good laughter?"

There were many kinds of laughter in her home

country, she had deciphered. There was the nervous-laughter, the shy-laughter, the good-fun-laughter, the laughter of children, the laughter of the sick. And the helpless laughter. When there's nothing else to do and tears are all evaporated into the clouds–and you laugh. There was never a short supply of laughter.

"Do you want to ask me about myself?"

"What was that?"

"Would you like to know what I've been doing?"

"Yes, yes. Very good."

"My studies are going well. I received high marks on my psychology exam."

"Very good. Yes, very good."

"And I think I've found the subject for my thesis."

"Your what?"

"Thesis. It's this long paper that I write using my own research. All doctors write them."

"Yes."

"Do you want to know about it?"

"Yes, I know."

"Anyway. I want to study how parental psychology differs between underdeveloped and developed countries. Are parents' habits different depending on the type of economic structure they hail from?"

"What does that mean? Habits?"

"The rules. The structure. What parents do every day. Routine."

"*Kea sheba*. I see."

"It's very interesting."

She didn't let her university friends visit her flat. She shared this space with a man—an art student who slept on the floor and let the milk go bad. He wasn't her boyfriend; in fact, he preferred men most of the time. But she couldn't tell her father about him.

The floor was covered in pieces of paper and Styrofoam and plastic dollhouse furniture—part of the installation he was working on. She cleaned the kitchen, the bathroom and her bedroom every day. The living room was his. But she had nothing. There was the one rug her grandmother had woven next to her mattress, but everything else was bare. Not like the colorful, woven-metallic, disarrayed, jumbled flats of her friends with their miniature furniture and plush bedding and pots, pans, wine racks, photographs and abstract art. They had garlic cloves hanging by the stove, bowls of mangoes and organic bananas, and fresh heads of lettuce, crispy French bread loaves. She kept a pot of porridge on the stove always, and heated it up when she was hungry. But being thin was glamorous here. Outside of her flat she was glamorous, but—

"You like it? Manchester?"

"Very much. It's a whole other world. You really should visit sometime." Though she knew he wouldn't, and she really didn't want him to.

"Yes. There are nicer things there. Cars and computers. Nicer things."

"Oh, yes. People even have computers on their mobiles. Brilliant idea."

"Computers are that little?"

"Can be." She didn't own a computer. She used one at the university lab. In the first two months of school she had seared herself to a computer screen and learned how to type, create a document, search the Internet. Her eyes had been bloodshot for weeks, and her wrists hurt. But she could use a computer.

"The Irish teacher says she can get a computer for the school. Though we will need a generator too."

Her father had been a principal once. Then he turned grey and now stumbled with a gnawed cane about the shop he owned.

"Where will you get the generator?"

"*Ach*, I don't know. This Irish teacher has a plan—grants, aid. Something with the government. She will get it."

"Best not put all of your hope in them."

"Who?"

She sighed. "Irish teachers."

"There is only one."

She trailed away from the window and over to the long, skinny mirror that hung from her door. She smoothed her shirt, her pants, while her father talked. "Actually, I need to get going."

"Going where?"

"To a party. It's my friend Felicia's birthday."

"Oh. We had a birthday party here the other day. For your nephew."

"Renang?"

"Hmm? Yes, Renang. He turned seven."

"Fourteen. He's fourteen now."

"What?"

"Fourteen. And his birthday was almost two months ago."

"Yes. We have not talked in awhile."

She had remembered to send Renang a card. A flashy one that when you opened it sang "Happy Birthday" in her recorded voice. "Did Renang get my card?"

"Card? Hmm…I don't think so."

It probably lay on the desk of some postal worker, stashed behind love letters and death notices and boxes of foreign aid.

"There should be one coming. I sent it out before…"

"Uh-huh." He wasn't listening anymore.

"So, I need to get ready for this party."

"Yes, yes. But first I need to tell you the news."

"News?" Why did he wait so long? As though phone cards were cheap.

"Ok, but you have to hurry. I'm almost out of time on my phone card."

"Card? I told you, we didn't get it yet—"

"Never mind. Tell me the news."

"We have a new teacher."

"What?"

"An Irish girl. A beautiful girl. She—"

"Da, you told me about her."

"I did?"

"Yes, already. You told me about her and the computer."

"The computer? I don't remember that."

"We did talk about it. Look, I have to go, the line is cutting out."

"You never ask me how I am."

She didn't know what to say. He was so blunt. "Sorry?"

"You never ask me how I am doing."

"God, Dad. Ok, how are you?"

"Oh, very fine. Very fine. Your mother though—"

"I know. Has a cough. I'm going to go now. But I will talk to you soon. Bye." She hung up, her father's shrill "buh-bye" hanging in her ears.

She sank to the bare floor. She had no party to go to. Felicia was out of town. Her roommate was at some art show in Berlin, so she had the place to herself.

She sat there, barefoot, and closed her eyes. She imagined the house of her parents and the cement floor and the dust that blew over everything, and the sounds of her parents–the sigh of her mother as she sat down, the scrape of her father's cane. There now–a chicken warbled outside the window–the glassless window that opened out onto the village yard–because it belonged to all. She imagined the wind and the sunshine and the smell of baking bread.

How They Spend Their Sundays

The dead car didn't have a steering wheel. Someone had sawed it off, so Seabata had rigged one out of chicken wire. Slight beneath his branchy fingers, it gave him the illusion that he could drive. Always driving at an angle, for one tire remained on the car, sunken and muddy. The others stripped by thieves.

Shorty lay on the floor of the car–the seats taken to sit in a hut–his feet bare and resting on the dash. He smoked a joint. It nestled in his wide white piano key teeth. He rubbed his fingers up and down his chest bone, playing his ribs.

"We could play football today."

"Nah." Seabata arched up and over the wheel, pretending that the road was getting steep. He wanted to be a driver, so he practiced in the hollows of dead cars.

The roads of Mafeteng were junkyards for abandoned objects and animals and body parts (for Ntate Fanthu's arm was found in a dried gulch, after a knife fight).

"I want to make break things. Like dinner plates. Make them out of clay and let them bake in the sun. Then break them over Lefu's head."

"He's a dumb fuck."

"Eh."

"But that sounds stupid. You say some stupid things,

Seabata."

"Shut up."

"You shut up."

"We could play football, you know. If you want."

Shorty kept smoking. The air in the car smelled of sheep and sweet dagga because all the windows were gone too.

They spent Sundays like this. After foot-stomping church when the village crept like ants into the schoolhouse and sang through lunchtime. Lunchtime was just a thought, fleeting, because Seabata hadn't eaten. If his older sister was less tired today, there might be the scrapings of dinner.

He had breakfast.

Shorty lived with his uncle a good hour away–his parents buried in a ditch in South Africa. He could see South Africa across the Lesotho border, but when he looked he didn't think about his parents. Their faces were two blurs, and all he could remember were their noses. His mother's was like three squashed grapes of the same ruddy purple color, his father's flat and wide, the nostrils high and black.

And that wasn't much to go on.

Though Seabata looked at his world through the emptiness where the windshield would have once been, he didn't really see the yellow rocks or the blue haze of South Africa. His eyes would still blink, but only in anticipation for the evening when he'd no longer have to see (and could just sleep).

Seabata was an orphan. He had a mother somewhere, and his father was dead from a time when billboards didn't tattoo their faces with warnings about AIDS. So he was only an orphan. But Shorty had neither parent, so the government liked to call him a double-orphan. But "double" made Shorty think of a lot of something, and he had nothing, and this just didn't seem right. His uncle liked to tell him, "You're a double-orphan, Shorty, and you've got nothing, so you've got to listen to me."

The boys had conversations of single thoughts.

"It's hot."

"I saw a white family the other day."

"I'm hungry."

"That bird is flying crazy."

They made an interesting pair: Shorty with his narrow waist and tiny-boned body, his skin inky and oily, his eyes big and wide like he was spooked. Seabata was tall and sort of leaned forward when he walked, his neck bent like the spout of a pitcher, his long, crooked jaw spilling towards the ground. His broad shoulders spread like wings, and his facial features were delicate and small, embedded in a sandy-colored face.

If they had the term best friends, this is what they would be.

Fuh-fuh-fuh. Shorty craned his neck out the open door. He watched the helicopter beat back the clouds, and the sky was borderless.

"If this car worked, how fast do you think it'd be against that airplane?"

"Helicopter, Shorty. It's called a helicopter." He didn't really know the difference, something about how they got into the air.

"Whatever. How fast you think it'd be?"

Seabata pulled out a memory from the trunk of his brain–when he had heard two taxi drivers talking. "I think a helicopter engine is bigger. It'd be a lot faster."

"I don't know," Shorty said. "Teboho drives his truck so fast, rocks fly."

"Well, if we knew where that helicopter was going, and we timed them, and then drove the same distance, we could figure it out. It's just algebra. Life algebra. You can use it."

Shorty rolled onto his stomach and threw the joint outside. It burned out slowly. "Aw, don't talk about that stupid algebra. We shouldn't have to think on the weekend."

Seabata hit his friend's thigh. "That's your problem, you don't ever think."

"I don't have to worry neither."

Seabata had little ridges in his forehead. He thought a lot about school and driving away and oceans he could float on and food shiny and sweet smelling.

Yelping children crowned the horizon. "Yoyo, Seabata!" one of the children called, his skinny frame a dark blot against the shivering sky. Clouds passed so quickly it seemed that the Earth was moving in double-time.

"It's your nephew, Seabata."

"That kid doesn't know when to leave me alone."

The two boys watched the nephew moving forward. He held onto a stick and chased the other kid–a sunny-faced girl that lived nearby. The girl ran towards the car and huddled by the open door. Shorty shoved her. "Whatcha doing?"

"He's chasing me."

When the nephew got closer, the boys could see a clot of feces covering the free end of the stick. "Stay back or I'll get you."

"Knock that off," muttered Seabata.

"Dontcha have anything better to do?" said Shorty, turning his head away at the stench.

"I'm being her boss. She's supposed to bring Seabata a message, 'me said. So I'm making sure she does."

The little girl giggled and held the bottom of her dress up to her mouth. Seabata turned around, taking his eyes off the imaginary road. "What message?" But the girl kept giggling until Shorty thumped her on the side of the head and the nephew jabbed the stick closer to her. Cornered, she managed to splutter, "A letter. Some school letter."

Seabata perked up. "Do you think it could be from St. Martin's?"

Shorty was uninterested. "Possibly."

Seabata–on a wave of excitement–had applied for admission to St. Martin's, the nicest boarding school in the district. If he could get in, he'd have a good shot at university. He could be both a driver and an engineer. Driving on the very roads and bridges he would design. In the holes of schooldays, he'd make himself invisible and sketch bridges over the ravines, steps down hillsides, train tracks across the border, and buildings so tall they shaded the sun.

"Did you bring the letter?"

The girl shook her head.

"Bad girl," the nephew said. "Let's go get it." He waved the shit-covered stick past her hairline, and she took off, back to the village. The nephew whooping behind her.

"Maybe I got in."

"Maybe."

"Don't get all excited. Maybe I didn't."

They sat in the afternoon noise without speaking.

"Seabata, we'll still be friends if you go to St. Martin's, right?"

"Sure. That's a dumb question."

"Yeah. It is."

The nephew and the girl didn't return. The boys talked about moving but didn't.

"Shorty! Seabata!" Each name spat from Lefu's throat. He went to school with them and was walking their way. He once tore the head off of a bird because he could. Not even for the wonder of it. Seabata got out of the car and faced Lefu–whose name meant death or sickness. Shorty–no matter what he said–liked Lefu, or liked being acknowledged by him, and, really, did it make any difference?

"Hey," Lefu croaked. Lefu's grandmother said the ancestors, who did not want him to escape the womb, had strangled his throat and this was why he had been named Lefu. Even as a baby he had cried in ghoulish rasps.

Shorty and Seabata nodded.

"You two want to come with? Some of us are accompanying Mokotsi. He is going to take Itumeleng."

"He wants her for his bride?" Shorty spit in the dirt.

"Yeah. She says she has refused him, but she's not going to get a better offer. And Mokotsi wants her."

Seabata sucked on his lower lip, he squatted down on the ground, avoiding Lefu's stern gaze. "The chief doesn't like bride-stealing. He says it's not modern, or Christian."

"Shit on him. It's custom. She doesn't know what's good for her."

"Maybe she doesn't like Mokotsi."

Lefu bent down and he smelled of wet sheep and heat. "Well, Mokotsi likes her. And it's a man's decision." Lefu wore a baseball jersey left by an aide worker. "Dan" was sewn on the breast, and sometimes he was jokingly called Lefu Dan. But only when he was in a good mood.

"We've got nothing else to do," said Shorty, because he and Seabata worked as a pair.

The sun grilled their bare foreheads as they cut through the turned up fields of the village. They headed towards the school. The school was a recently built cement box with a fine, sloping red roof (Seabata noted) and glass windows so freshly blown that they still carried the heat of the fires. There were no desks and only a smattering of shocking-blue plastic chairs. The blackboards were blown over with chalk-dust, the erasers hidden in teachers' homes. Chalk stubs scattered about the floor, under desks, having dropped from children's mouths. They ate chalk to feed their bellies, gain some vitamins.

The three boys entered the first classroom, the one belonging to the younger Form A students (of which Itumeleng was a part) and waited, leaning against the walls. From beyond the windows they heard a shriek carried on the back of the breeze, and the scuffling of feet.

"Open it," Mokotsi called, and Lefu propped open the door. Mokotsi and another boy dragged Itumeleng into the classroom.

Seabata hadn't talked to Itumeleng much before. And he had thought of her as an underfed girl–flat everywhere, except her thick calves and ankles–and with a perfectly oval-shaped face. It was so perfect because her ears were so tiny and pressed against her head, almost like they were invisible. Seabata couldn't look at her face.

"Shut it," ordered Mokotsi. The capture had already occurred. As Itumeleng fought–kicked at them, dug her nails into the boys' forearms–Mokotsi explained that they found her wandering towards the school and were able to follow her. The other boy was Mokotsi's half-brother–a stupid, good-looking man (for he was nearly twenty-two and still stuck in the Form C class with all of the other boys). Seabata had once spied on the half-brother kissing the neck of his sister, Agnes. They were nearly the same age.

The half-brother held onto Itumeleng's arms, pulling her elbows closer together. She moaned and swung her hips back and forth, creating momentum to loosen his grasp. She attempted a head butt, and Mokotsi yelled for someone to grab onto her ankles. Shorty dove, and Lefu got on the ground to help him. She was pinned, and her towel–a ratty, pink thing she had tied around her waist like a skirt–came undone, and Seabata saw that she wore tight pants underneath. He could make out each of her thighs, and they met somewhere up in the black V of women.

Mokotsi grabbed Seabata's shoulder. "Be our watch. If anyone comes, knock three times."

"You have her," Seabata choked. He kept his voice low in the turmoil of her crying and the boys' gruff insults. "She's yours now."

"Not enough, Seabata." Mokotsi's eyes were like two pale, dead fish, the pupils sunk in their stomachs. "Now watch."

The door didn't lock, so Seabata leaned against it. No one would come by on a Sunday. Before him was the schoolyard, patiently quiet. Behind the door he heard Itumeleng's kicks, muffled screams, and the undoing of belts. When the groans and ragged breathing–like rasping, running dogs–got too loud, he scuttled away from the door and sat in the middle of the yard, wishing for someone to come.

When Seabata returned home, his sister Agnes was on the front stoop. She was listening to the radio from the house next-door, sipping watered-down chicory coffee.

"I've got your letter right here," she said first thing. The thin brown envelope rested on her lap, and Seabata knew she would have opened it and read the contents, then folded it up neatly and had probably been sitting here since dinnertime, anticipating Seabata's return, so she could read it again.

"Who's it from?"

"Didn't read it." And she handed it to him.

The letter was typed on stiff paper with a seal. In formal words it told Seabata that he was admitted for the following term to St. Martin's.

"I got in."

"That's good work. You work hard." Agnes took the letter and folded it up, putting it gently into its envelope. "And they're giving you a scholarship too?"

He nodded and sat next to her. The sun burned low to the horizon, and the good feeling of the booming music next door only made Seabata sad.

"You don't seem too happy. You should be clapping and smiling. Something, Seabata." Agnes watched him with a mother's awareness.

"I'm tired is all."

She patted his hand, but he moved away and into the house, the radio singing behind him.

Seabata awoke the next morning with a headache. He left the house early, when Agnes was just starting to cook the lesheleshele, and avoided talking any more about the letter. He went to the road, by the phone shop, but continued walking towards the school rather than waiting for Shorty.

Seabata expected the school to be different. He wasn't sure exactly how he expected it to be—maybe like a thin veil of cobwebs you suddenly recognized in corners. He wanted to push past them. But the silk of yesterday still clung to him.

Mokotsi was absent, and his half-brother came in late, with Shorty. The teacher beat them at lunchtime for tardiness, while Seabata watched over his food. During math, he went to the toilet and on coming back, peered into the Form A classroom. One window was partially opened. He hadn't seen Itumeleng all day, and he studied the heads of the young ones but couldn't find her. The classroom was filled now with paper-chomping from still-hungry kids and the teacher's drone of science facts. He heard a few girls closest to the window giggling.

Yesterday, Itumeleng had not giggled, and Seabata had not watched through the window as he did now. He had pieced together the history of that event by the sounds he heard coming from the classroom. He knew what they had done, and it made him sick. Then he thought about what Itumeleng must have done afterwards. The boys had come out, sweaty and slightly angry, a bit of pleasure seeping from their glares. Shorty had his pants undone, and he buttoned them up as he told Seabata they better get going. The boys talked about getting her back to Mokotsi's place–about Mokotsi maybe not wanting her now–and Seabata slid closer to the window. He saw the shadow of Itumeleng crouched on the ground, simultaneously holding her stomach and reaching for her pants. Seabata couldn't stop watching her and all he heard was soft crying, and when he couldn't stand it anymore, he fled, Shorty shouting after him, "Hey! Seabata? Seabata?"

He let Shorty walk home with him after school. Shorty walked close to him, and Seabata could feel the breath of his skin.

"You haven't been talking much today."

Seabata shrugged. "Not much to talk about."

"Did you get your letter?"

"Yeah. I got in."

"No shit." Shorty punched his arm, but Seabata just kept walking. "Man, how about that? So you're going to go?"

"I guess so."

"You guess so?" Shorty laughed, but Seabata was straight-faced. "Would sure beat this place."

"Yeah, it would."

They came up to the phone shop, a dingy metal shack with a big logo on the front–a splotch of blue and yellow that blinked in the sinking sunlight. "Need to make a call?" a man in the stall called out.

The boys passed by, splitting their paths as they did every afternoon.

The next day, everyone at school had heard about Itumeleng. The teachers spoke about it in huddled whispers but passed the boys as if they were unseen. The students chattered in clusters and yet asked no questions of them. Classes progressed as normal, minus Itumeleng. Mokotsi had returned, and he and his half-brother sat in the back of the Form C class and didn't do their work. The teachers came in and out, teaching their subjects, but didn't walk to the back of the room. When Mokotsi launched a paper ball at Neo's head in the front of the room, the English teacher walked around the girl but didn't say anything.

At lunch, Mokotsi and his half-brother cornered

Seabata in the classroom. The half-brother sat on his desk, and Mokotsi leaned over Seabata's back, breathing into his ear. "You've been doing some talking. Haven't you, Seabata?"

He said nothing. Because he knew Mokotsi didn't want to listen to him. The half-brother sneered and picked up Seabata's pencil and jabbed the point onto the table, millimeters from Seabata's hand. The pencil tip broke, and he rolled the pencil across the desk; it fell onto Seabata's lap.

"Brother, you remember what happened to Ntate's arm? Be something bad if Seabata lost an arm, wouldn't it?"

The classroom door creaked open. "Hey, guys." Shorty stood in the doorway. "Guys, leave him alone."

"Your friend's a snake. Telling lies about that girl."

"That girl is named Itumeleng," Seabata mumbled.

Mokotsi pulled at Seabata's shirt. "Talking again, huh?"

"Stop." Shorty didn't move any closer. His hand still rested on the door handle. "Look, Mokotsi, Seabata didn't say anything."

"How do you——"

"I know, ok? Besides, if Seabata talks, he'll be in trouble too. I heard Itumeleng or her sister or someone's been saying something."

"This true?"

Seabata looked at Shorty, whose eyes got even bigger,

and he slightly nodded his head. "Yeah, I didn't say anything."

"Get out of here," Mokotsi told him.

Seabata moved slowly out of his chair, kept an eye on the half-brother's hands. His pencil pinged against the ground. He moved past Shorty and away from the crowd at the kitchen, past the staff workroom, where one teacher lazily watched him from a window and banged against the pane at Seabata when he kept on walking. He walked in his loping, long-legged manner all the way home. He didn't stop until he got to his stoop and collapsed by Agnes' feet and told her, "I'm going to St. Martin's this week."

He never thought he would be considered guilty. By that evening, the whole village had heard, and there was talk that a police officer might be visiting the school and questioning the boys. Agnes went into her room and cried. The nephew kept saying, "What happened? What happened?"

Seabata crouched by the door of her room. "I didn't do anything, Agnes." He waited for her to come out. The nephew scrounged in the kitchen, eating congealed lesheleshele that he scraped from the breakfast pot. When Agnes did finally come out, Seabata stayed kneeling by her feet. "I swear I didn't do anything."

She brushed past him. "That's the problem."

Seabata didn't go back to school. He stayed at home,

waiting until the Saturday bus could take him to St. Martin's. He packed his few belongings–his school uniform, two changes of clothes, a deck of playing cards and a visor–into a flowered suitcase that Agnes lent him.

In the middle of the week, he went to use the toilet, and a police officer was standing in front of the outhouse.

"Seabata Thejane?"

"Eh, ntate."

"I have questions for you."

"Ntate?" Seabata pointed to the outhouse, and the officer stepped aside. Seabata went into the outhouse. Black widows crawled out from the seat lid, and he beat them down into the hole in the ground.

The officer's voice on the other side of the tin door re-created the muffled intimacy of telephone conversations. Seabata could see his gun holster from the crack between door and doorframe.

"Are you a friend of Mokotsi Mokoena?"

"No, ntate. We go to school together."

"Do you know a girl by the name of Itumeleng 'Moosa?"

"She goes to my school, but I've never spoken to her."

"Did you boys hurt her?"

"I never touched her, ntate."

The officer tapped the door. "You sure?"

"Eh." There was a stack of old newspapers by Seabata's feet. He tore one of the papers, right through the Queen's face, and used it to wipe. He opened the door when he was finished, and the officer watched him. Seabata saw Agnes standing on the stoop. He averted his eyes from the officer's.

"Hey," the officer said. "I heard you are going to St. Martin's?"

"Eh, ntate."

"Go well." The officer left him standing there.

That night Seabata heard from the neighbor—a brash woman who gossiped with the windows open—that the boys weren't talking, that Itumeleng (or her sister or aunt or someone) had only identified Mokotsi. The chief threatened to whip him. Lefu had disappeared, but no one seemed too concerned.

"I'm going for a walk," Seabata told Agnes when he couldn't take the gossip anymore. The roads were abuzz with snippets of facts and slabs of lies about what had happened to Itumeleng. An old man by the phone shop spit tobacco in front of Seabata's feet, but he just nodded and kept walking. These stores and houses and ditches filled with children and trash would no longer be his when he left the next morning. He'd go to St. Martin's and would only come back during holiday. And, then, only as a visitor.

Itumeleng lived with her family by the main road, just down the way from the small Indian restaurant that Seabata had never been in. The blue roof of her house was achingly cheerful. Across the road, two men were selling tomatoes, onions, and cabbages out of an old donkey cart, and Seabata pretended to be looking at them as he watched Itumeleng's house. He didn't know what he expected to see. He heard that Itumeleng wouldn't be coming back to school, and, as far as he knew, no one had seen her outdoors since Sunday.

"Move along boy," the cart owners said when Seabata had been there too long, fondling a tomato to the point of bruising it.

He walked home, cutting through the back lot of the Indian restaurant. He picked up the butt of a still-hot cigarette that a restaurant worker must have tossed from the kitchen door. He inhaled, and for a moment he felt like he couldn't breathe and that if maybe he held it in long enough he would choke to death. Instead, he sputtered.

The short way home led him to the dead car, and he climbed in and spread himself out in the back seat, staring at the rusted, peeled away top and smoked. He fell asleep like that.

Agnes handed him his suitcase the next morning. And a plastic sack with two slices of bread and a hard-boiled egg. She touched him gently on the cheek and then pushed him out the door. The nephew cried in a corner. "Go well, Seabata," Agnes said.

The sun had just crested over the horizon line when Seabata got to the bus stop. There was a gathering of people waiting already, propped on their bags, rubbing sleep from their eyes.

Shorty was walking towards Seabata. "Hey." He sounded friendly. "Heard you were leaving today, thought I'd come say goodbye."

"How you've been, Shorty?"

Shorty waved his hands. "So-so. They brought a policeman, did you hear? Asked me questions, but I told them I had nothing."

"That's what you said?"

"Well," he grinned. "And that Mokotsi wanted a bride. The policeman didn't say much, but the chief said Mokotsi will probably get sent to a tribunal. Mokotsi's mother wailed all last night." He plugged his ears with his fingers as though her wails had carried this far. "Could barely sleep."

"I see."

Shorty scuffed his shoes along the dirt road. "School won't be the same without you." Neither of them mentioned that school hadn't been the same all week. "Who's gonna help me with my homework?"

"Maybe you'll just talk the teachers into passing you."

Shorty looked at him strangely. "Don't hide yourself at St. Martin's, Seabata."

"I won't."

There would be no letters or phone calls from post offices. No visits or random taxi sightings. For beyond this they would not know each other.

"The taxi's getting full."

"I should buy some fat cakes."

"It's hot today."

"I should sit down now."

Seabata reached out his hand, and Shorty took it. They clasped each other's hands in the three-clasp handshake. "See you around."

On the surface they looked past each other's chins and nodded and shook hands, but underneath…

"See you around.

The Secrets of Mothers and Daughters

His face looked like death. I saw the lesions first. Tacked to his skin like charred leeches, dripping pus. I couldn't vomit in front of him.

There he was: a peeled apart version of the man simply known as my father. He was a man knocked apart and carelessly rebuilt. First it had stripped his appetite, leaving the skin in rows of dried petals sewn onto the bones that had been gnawed away. These bones (they had carried my brothers and sisters, had worked in fields, driven cattle) had been twisted apart from the joints, the blood drained from his face, his gums gored and left weeping blood.

And here in hospital they put him back together.

Attached the bones and wove the blood back into the veins, sewed the skin petals back into place. Though I could still see the seams. They left him unfamiliar. For doctors are not artists but patch workers. And grandmothers darn quilts better than they heal bodies.

"Water."

And I held the straw up to his lips, which had been stretched and molded into a ridge, damming up around his endless black mouth.

I said hello to the first white man I met. I bought my first Western suit for the second wedding I had–to a thin girl with braids. She cut them off on our wedding night.

I had a life of many wedding nights. I had only one night with her mother. In a mining town. And the sky around us was a black hole. Except for where the moon broke through to lead her home.

Hospital was his new home now. And the floor next to his bed might as well have been mine. Some nights he would almost stop breathing, and I would stay on the floor–the dirty tile cool on my cheeks–my blanket under my head. Waiting for him to breathe. He would wake up before the sun stretched over the buildings, and I would talk to him. Tell him what he was missing in the world beyond nurses and medicine schedules.

"The Queen had a prince. Isn't that a great thing for the country?" That happened a year ago, but his eyes brightened every time.

"I bought a mango in the market. As big as my head. And when I cut it open the flesh burst like the sun and inside was a gold coin." Neither of us had seen real gold before but he liked this. "Pretty gold." He spoke in words, not thoughts or sentences. Like a baby learning to speak. Or a tourist trying to blend in.

"Mufasa had to carry a sheep on his back in order to bring it to the wedding celebration of his niece. The taxi broke down and lightning put it on fire, so he had to walk. They say the sheep watched the fire from behind

Mufasa's back, and the flames mesmerized it. It died from beauty before he reached the celebration."

"Sheep meat."

"Yes, when your teeth grow back I'll cook you a sheep."

If teeth grew like aloe plants, they'd be baby stumps after three months, full smooth teeth by six, and dead and fallen out by nine. We could eat all the sweets we desired, because after a year we'd have a fresh batch to chew and chomp and gleam in strands of smiles.

If teeth grew like beets then I'd wait until harvest and grow back the tooth that had been knocked out of my head when I was twelve. And if I were generous, I'd let him grow his back as well.

She bit my ear when we made love, and I like to think there's a bit of a scar there. She gave me a scar and a child, and that's the end. I have many scars—her love bite; the scar from the knife fight when I was a buck; the one when they cut me open and took out my burst appendix; the one from the hoe, when it came down on my foot.

I have many scars. I also have many children. And they are harder to ignore.

A parent can have many children, and they can choose to speak to the ones they please, feed those better that they love, live with those if the mood suits them. But a child only has two parents. And if one drifted away like an untied boat, and the other doesn't want you, then what do you do?

You visit them when they are dying and make them remember. Make them want you.

I remember these things: sneaking into the dam and being clean for the only time ever in my life; dropping my eldest son and his crying; the feel of my first woman; the feel of the last; scoring the winning goal in the seventh form football championship; driving; buying my first cow and watching it die from stomach infection; the burning fields; eating at the KFC; spending my first maluti. Getting sick. Watching the bike race in the capital city; falling...blacking out; the hospital; her face; the hospital...

I avoided looking at his face. This was easy. From the earliest days in school we stared beyond the teachers' heads: at their necks, the ground, above their eyebrows. But I wanted to look. And I thought about it as he slept.

Maybe the others will have arrived while he slept. The eldest with his fat stomach and two wives. Mufasa who had a yellow mother and a younger brother who refused to meet me. Or the twins; they were beautiful and because they were the only other daughters (and from his second wife, the favorite) they were Lintle 1 and Lintle 2. So we will always know that they were beautiful. Lintle 1 wouldn't let me in her house. She slapped me on the street for calling him my father. But how else could I have told her the news?

Lintle 2 had a lazy eye (and that was why she was 2).

But she baked me cookies and wrapped them in magazine papers, so I could read the stories and tape the pictures to my outhouse walls. But she wouldn't come either. Said that the babies would be frightened. I didn't tell her not to bring the babies. Excuses came easy to us. That was how we survived.

I survived a drowning. A baby lamb had gotten caught in a current in the summer. Drought was only a scrapbook memory. I went to save it and slipped on a rock. My ears filled with water. I remember the wet silence the most. I couldn't swim. Only fishes do that. It was the first of two times I stopped breathing. Someone pulled me up. The second time I stopped breathing was when I was sick and fell. Breathing is hard to hang on to, like money or women. Gone quickly before you really appreciate it.

"You took life for granted," the priest told him. He had come to pray with my father who knew no prayers. Maybe that was why God chose him to die? We were all chosen, I supposed, but He might have decided to kill you by drowning or fire or guns or childbirth. Or disease. There was always disease here.

The priest smelled of curry, and there were little foamy bits of spit on his lips as he spoke: "Our Father, who art in heaven…"

And I said my own prayer because Mother Joan at the school I went to said that as long as you were sincere– and God would know it if you weren't–He would hear you. I left God behind when I left school. But he was coughing and his ribs were rickety boards of a bridge over his heart–if it hadn't shriveled–and the priest in black muttered over a rosary for that same godless heart. And I took Him up again.

And I said in my head, "My father, soon to be in heaven, when you get there–if you get there–you'll know what I think about you. And I'm sorry God for what I think, when all I want to do is to feel love. Help me feel love."

The priest chattered in rhythm with the beads. "Amen." He watched my lips. "Do you have anything you would like to say?"

I shook my head. That was a question that he did not want the answer to.

"May God save his soul."

If God really was in the soul-saving business, then I had better become his customer.

I stood in line at the ATM the week before I fell. She had come for money. There was no more school for her. There had been so many children before her; there wasn't any money. But every other week she showed up for something. And every other week I would go to the ATM and try to pull out money and tell her, "No, not any money this week." This wasn't always a lie.

From somewhere outside my head, I heard a man's voice telling me to ask for forgiveness.

I ask for forgiveness.

The one time I saw my mother, she crouched on the ground near my head where I slept and asked me to forgive her. I knew it was her because I could smell her milk. She told me his name and where I could find him and gave me a red handkerchief that she said he would remember.

"You could have his eyes," she told me, and they *were* funny and almond-colored.

His eyes were pasty now. Any color had been eaten away, but I didn't look at them long.

Mother had said, "Never, ever bring this up again. This is our secret. The secret of mothers and daughters."

It was all my mother gave me. That and his handkerchief. Then she vanished in the pickup of another man.

"Any time now," the nurse told me. She sailed in and out of the hospital room every few hours. Still, I foolishly waited for the others to come. I didn't have a phone, but I wrote four notes, and the nurse said she would send them out. I'm pretty sure she just crumpled them up and pushed them into her pockets. I saw the bulges there the next time she came into the room with the cup of medicine.

I kept hard candies in my pocket. I would give them to all of the children—and then the grandchildren. Every time I saw her I would give her one. And she would smile only out of the corner of her mouth. *I did that for her.*

By God, I did that.

There was nothing for anyone to do. But I continued to sit, to sleep by his bed, to hand him his water.

My memories of him will be boxed up in his coffin. The conversations nailed away, the hateful thoughts buried underground.

I chose the spot where I want to be buried. It is on a mound behind the home of my ancestors. But there is so little body for them to bury. I can't feel my arms anymore. And out of the hole in my head, I looked up and saw—her.

Had she been here all along? She leaned over, and I saw the shadow of her mother who I had bought for coins one night. I needed to tell her in that moment, as gray, feathery shapes began to hide my eyes.

"I love you," I tried to say. "Daughter, I love you." She needed to hear it once. Once is all it takes.

He gargled. "Lovey." I thought I could make that out. But whenever had he used the word love? His drowned-out unreadable eyes looked at me. This time I looked back.

The nurse said, "He sees you. I'll leave you to say something." She was gone, though I knew she'd be lurking near the door. A dead body would be a day's work done.

I stood up and leaned over him. The only image of my mother floated beside me. That night when she told me that this man–the man decomposing before me–might be my father. And he might not. But either way, I should give it a shot. Because she didn't want to stay with me.

So I told him: "I am not your daughter." I presented that like a flag of truce. Like a sin in confession. Like a cow to a bridegroom. It was my last word–my last secret–my last gift.

His mouth sagged open and stiffened. I walked out of the room. They would bury him in the morning.

The Mountains Are Watching

Madam Phalatsi chose a thin barely blossoming branch from the tree in the schoolyard.

"Nthibeleng. *Tlo koana.* Come here."

The school was at assembly, and the students stood in their respective forms, facing the row of teachers in front of the staff room. They tittered nervously as a small, plump girl from Form C walked to the front, her hands clasped behind her back, her eyes roving between her classmates and the ground.

"She is sleeping with the boys," Madam Phalatsi had explained to Amanda right before assembly. The boys she referred to were mysteriously absent.

"Maybe we shouldn't beat her, Madam," Amanda had replied, prepared to use her foreignness to take a stand against outdated Basotho custom.

Madam Phalatsi avoided Amanda's stare through sleepy eyelids. "In Lesotho, these students do not have respect."

"And you will beat respect into them, Madam?"

The headmistress had turned away, her braided head bowed towards her chest.

Madam Phalatsi muttered accusations in a flowing mix of Sesotho and English at Nthibeleng's shaved head. Amanda turned her head away, refusing to watch.

Hwoop, hwoop, hwoop, hwoop—the branch flicked the air and violently slapped Nthibeleng's open palm. Once for each boy. Madam Phalatsi passed the switch to Sir Mothepu and Sir Lereko and finally to Madam Mampho. They each whipped Nthibeleng four times. Amanda turned and went inside the staff room.

Birds clicked on top of the metal roof of the staff room as Amanda collected her books for the first English class of the day. Madam Phalatsi disappeared into her makeshift office. A tumbled down door and plywood wall built in haste were all that separated her from the teachers. Lereko and Mothepu sat at the desk they shared; Lereko looked through two-week old tests that he still hadn't marked while Mothepu nestled into his folded arms and took a nap. Mampho shared a desk with Amanda—Amanda's side unorganized with stacks of books and lesson plans and markers and stickers scattered about like a pulled-apart rainbow. Mampho, the math teacher, was orderly. Her barely-opened books were straightened and her pens lined up. She stared out the window, a crumpled tissue in her lap. She had a sinus infection that never went away.

Classes began and ended with Amanda. There had been a bell, but some mischievous student had stolen it, and the battery in the school clock had long since died. It was up to Amanda and her Timex to start classes.

Amanda's first class was the Form Cs. An American equivalent of tenth grade, her students ranged from ages sixteen to twenty-two with Mokoto Naha as her oldest and little Nthibeleng—who now sucked on her sore palm—the youngest. Amanda's first year volunteering in Ha Lithaba was coming to a close. She was halfway through her service in Lesotho but still felt as though she hadn't made the slightest imprint upon her school.

Twenty Form Cs crowded around nine broken, crooked desks worn and wrinkled by carvings and pen scratches. The cement floor was cracked with tiny gullies and a lone chalkboard hung on the uneven wall. The students wore uniforms of faded ocean blue with skirts and black torn tights for the girls and dirty khaki pants for the boys. In the beginning, tucked behind their desks, Amanda had trouble telling the students apart. All of them had their heads shaved as an equalizer and protector against lice. Now, Amanda felt ashamed that she had been that naïve, that…white. Their faces—round, long, bony—flashed shades of chocolate and mocha, dirt-black and honey, each varying and unique.

One Sunday (when the village was at church and she waited for her clothes to dry on the line) Amanda had flipped through old copies of Vogue that her sister kept sending her and tore out pictures of models and celebrities and cut away their hair. She lined up the pictures and examined them. Without hair or makeup or sexually biased clothing, even flour-faced white Americans looked androgynous. There was a stronger, albeit subtler, beauty to the androgyny of her students, like they had descended from the first humans. Amanda imagined that this is what Adam and Eve must've looked like: colorful and sexually unidentifiable, for wasn't Eve a version of Adam? Equally beautiful and raw?

Amanda smiled at Nthibeleng, who shyly smiled back, then tucked her chin into her chest. "Take out your novels," Amanda instructed. With the national exams less than a month away, Amanda knew that the class needed to reread the poorly written book. The Form Cs would have to write an essay on it, but they could barely remember what happened in chapter one.

Nthibeleng read aloud. While she read, the others gazed out the window at a dismal scene of dry mountains and herdboys leading a scraggly band of sheep down the ravine, the riverbed dried up and barren. Only one student paid any attention. When Mokoto Naha wasn't reading, he'd follow the words with the tip of his ruler and mouth the words like a small child. If a student stumbled over a word or drifted into silence because he or she had no idea even how to begin to pronounce liaison, for example, Mokoto would loudly correct or aid a student. And, when it was even hard for Mokoto to pay attention, he would visually follow Amanda's movements about the room.

As the oldest student, Mokoto's education meant a bit more to him. He was Amanda's best student–dutiful, inquisitive, quick. Mokoto was the first student whose name Amanda learned. He was striking and very tall for

Basotho (though Madam Mampho had told Amanda that Mokoto's dead mother may have been part Zulu). He had dark brown skin and teeth so white they seemed painted between his lips. He'd often grin—slow and unfurling like flower petals. When the class grew bored or stared at Amanda in a mix of confusion and blankness, Amanda would catch Mokoto's eye for reassurance that she made sense—that someone got it. He would raise his eyebrows and jerk his head in a kind of half-nod, acknowledging that he heard her. That he and he alone understood.

Amanda also fully admitted to herself that Mokoto was her favorite.

"Mokoto loves you, Madam," the Form C girls teased. "He wants to marry you."

Amanda would laugh. "Oh, I'm so old," she'd sigh dramatically and pretend to hobble across the room. The class would laugh too and scream in enthusiasm.

"No, Madam, you're not old."

And she wasn't. Amanda was only twenty-three, a year older than Mokoto. In the village, Amanda was approached by men of all ages. "Marry me," they'd declare, half in jest, half serious, grabbing her hands, touching her hair—almost blonde and bone-white at the tips.

But Mokoto and the other Form C boys were on the cusp. Neither boy nor man. In their homes and the village, they were *ntate*, man, some engaged to much younger girls, others leading parentless families. Mokoto–with no parents–lived with his aunt and cousins. But in school they were *abuti* or boy. Mokoto would play soccer and steal Nthibeleng's pen and look doe-eyed at Amanda as he stammered out English greetings but be expected to help in the fields and feed his cousins when he got home.

Mokoto worked hard to please Amanda, and he complimented her daily. "You look nice, Madam," he'd say. But she just dismissed it as a childish crush.

Only Mokoto wasn't a child.

Amanda ate lunch in the staff room. The Form B girls dished up plates of *papa* and *moroho*–boiled maize meal and oil-soaked spinach–for each of the teachers. An old village woman cooked the food on open fires. The students would line up with their chipped metal bowls and receive smaller portions. But Madam Phalatsi wasn't letting them eat that day.

For the past two days, the older boys had taken second and third helpings leaving the younger boys and most of the girls without anything to eat. Madam Phalatsi decided to punish all of them. Only the teachers would eat today.

Amanda picked at her food. Day in and day out she ate the tasteless *papa* and *moroho*, but today it was almost bitter with her guilt. She nodded at one of the serving girls, Palesa, to take away her plate. She knew that Palesa would hide behind the staff room and gobble the food, hunched over and protecting it from the rest of the hungry students.

"*Koko.*" Someone knocked on the door.

"Come in," Amanda said. Schools were supposed to be English-speaking, but Amanda was the only one who followed that rule.

Mokoto walked in. "Good morning," he said to all of the teachers although it was almost one in the afternoon. He avoided their stares out of respect. He stood in front of Amanda's desk, a sign that he wanted something.

"Yes, Mokoto?"

"Um, Madam…" He paused to compose himself and to think about what he wanted to say. This wasn't a sign of being dumb because whenever Mokoto spoke, he spoke well–clearly–with a lisp of a British accent, a remnant of a past native-English teacher.

The other teachers began to laugh. "Cat got your tongue," Mampho jeered.

Amanda tried to catch Mokoto's eye, and she smiled– small and private just for him. "Do you have a question?"

"Yes, Madam." He fingered her stacks of books. His fingernails were like pale pink whittled seashells against his brown skin. "Could you help me study for the English exam?"

"When Mokoto?"

"Before school, Madam. Tomorrow."

"Why not after school?" Amanda's mornings were precious. She would sleep in, basking in the quiet that was stolen from her once the school hours were in play.

"I have to help my aunt in the fields." He watched her.

School began at 7:45. It took Amanda fifteen minutes to get to school—down the mountainside and across the riverbed. They'd have to meet at seven sharp to get anything done.

"If it's a problem, Madam, then you can say no."

"No. It isn't a problem."

He grinned, relieved. "I will meet you tomorrow."

"At my house, ok?" Amanda's house was warmer and on Mokoto's way to school. Inviting him to her house made it seem like he was a guest. And Amanda had few guests.

"Ok. Thank you, Madam."

Mampho walked home with Amanda. They lived down the main road from each other, got water from the same tap, bought flour from the same cinderblock shop.

"Did you listen to the radio yesterday?" Mampho asked.

"No," Amanda replied, because she was pretty sure Mampho didn't mean the BBC.

"A school in Mafeteng had a riot. The students stabbed their principal."

"What? That's crazy. Why?"

"*Ach*, I don't know. They did not like him. He beat the students badly."

106

"How scary." Amanda shook her head, grateful—at this moment at least—to be tucked away in the rural, relatively safe mountains. Mafeteng was near the border—and big—and scary. Amanda had only been there once, and a taxi driver had grabbed her arm through a van window and punched her shoulder angrily. All because she had refused to ride in his taxi.

"Mafeteng is dangerous," Mampho agreed. "Not like here. Here in Ha Lithaba it is peaceful."

Amanda thought of Nthibeleng. "What are you doing this weekend, Mampho?"

Mampho smiled. "I'm going to Maseru to visit my husband."

Mampho's husband worked in the capitol city at a textile factory as a manager. She smiled with a mix of pride and bashful love.

"I need to go into the camptown for some groceries. Maybe we will be on the same taxi into town?"

"Yes," Mampho said happily. She touched Amanda's wrist with lazy fingers. "See you tomorrow."

Amanda wanted to invite Mampho to her home, but the last time Mampho came by for tea, she had asked to keep Amanda's CD player and then stuffed half a package of biscuits in her coat pockets. Amanda had pretended not to notice.

It was September, but the chilly aftermath of winter still hung inside Amanda's *rondavel*. It seeped through the cement walls and thatched roof and hovered about her. Her floor heater was out of gas, and it was a pain to drag the tank into town on the taxi, so she kept her wool coat on as she fixed dinner: spaghetti noodles and margarine. She turned on her short wave radio and tuned it to a South African station. They didn't mention the riots.

Her tabby kitten Muriel uncurled herself from Amanda's sleeping bag to wind around Amanda's ankles. Other American volunteers gave their pets Sesotho names—embracing the language, the culture. But Amanda suited herself to an absurdly old-fashioned English name because she thought it created a bond with her cat. Muriel had a double-duty of keeping out the mice and keeping Amanda company. Amanda would tell Muriel about her day, read her letters aloud while stroking the cat's ears, and sing Christmas carols to her while they fell asleep at night.

It had been two months since Amanda had seen another volunteer. Taxi strikes were making travel outside of her district impossible. The nearest volunteer was a six-hour walk away. Luckily, Amanda had a mobile phone —a cheap Motorola—and when the days weren't windy (which was rare) and if she stood on a chair near the east-facing window, she could get decent reception. Her parents hadn't called in seven weeks. She hadn't gotten mail in almost eight.

Amanda, upon college graduation, had wanted to save the world. Or, less idealistically, change it in some small, yet significant way. Contribute to global progression. But instead the world had shut her up and out, alone in a dry, desolate country that most people had never heard of. There was always the possibility of escape (and she felt guilty sometimes that she had that when her students didn't), but she didn't want to be a failure. She wasn't always sure if she meant a failure to her students, to her family back home, to herself.

If Amanda sat real still and all she heard was the lonely wail of the mountain winds, then she almost believed the fantasy that she was the last person on Earth. And during the quiet quake of those moments, Amanda cried. Because feeling something was better than feeling like nothing at all.

The next morning she fried eggs, hand-picked from the school chickens. She wore her black skirt from the day before and a nubby sweater that she hadn't washed in a month. Her hair was pulled back in the standard ponytail. Her face tingled with cold, mountain water freshness. She had woken up early to fill her bucket with water to wash and boil for drinking. The drought had lifted, yet Amanda still used water sparingly.

"*Koko!*"

"*Ema hanyane.* Just a minute." Amanda put her dishes into the washtub. Other than school, she made a point never to eat in front of her half-starved students.

Amanda opened the door and unlocked the burglar

bars that protected all volunteers. With a thin, battered satchel slung across his shoulders, Mokoto stood away from the door.

Amanda let him in. "Good morning, Mokoto."

"I didn't come for English," Mokoto explained, sitting down at her table. He took out his math book. "Madam Mampho does not explain algebra well. You can help me?"

Amanda grinned. "Sure. Let's take a look."

They worked for the next half hour on quadratic equations. Mokoto wrote his figures neatly and followed Amanda's finger as she pointed out problems and gave him examples. He frowned and sucked on his bottom lip as he worked.

Mokoto learned quickly. Amanda's voice was high and sweet but firm, a balance she naturally had and which worked well with her students. Mokoto asked her questions, drifting from algebra to the pictures on her wall, then about her home in America. He had asked her questions before—in class—but it was more personal when he sat next to her, the scent of her lotion wafting from her skin.

Amanda played with the chunky, silver ring she always wore, moving it from one hand to the other, twisting it in her fingers, as if by touching it she steadied herself. Then Mokoto took her hand, and she stopped talking. He covered her hand with both of his and blew on it gently and kissed it. For a second, she wondered if he had ever touched a white hand before.

She pulled away. "What are you doing, Mokoto?"

"I'm sorry, Madam." He couldn't look at Amanda, so he gathered his books and left.

Amanda waited until Mokoto had disappeared down the hill to start out for school. Her hand itched with his touch.

"This isn't happening. It was nothing. It was nothing."

A herdboy, dirty and dressed in a grey blanket and loose cap, laughed at her. She always talked to herself aloud, craving any conversation in her realm of loneliness.

When Amanda arrived at school, the morning assembly was over. The students stood in clumps near the classrooms, the kitchen, the toilets.

"Hey," she yelled to one Form A—a brazen beautiful girl named Kananelo. "Get inside your classrooms. It's after 8:00."

Kananelo shrugged. "Madam Phalatsi is not here. The teachers are not teaching."

Amanda herded the students into their classrooms. She didn't teach until second period, but she gave them all writing exercises to keep them busy.

The Form As were quick and eager and, ready to start, burrowed into their desks. The Form Bs, bored and disinterested, played cards, ignoring Amanda's instructions. Frustrated, she went to the Form Cs to give them a sample essay to help them prep for the national exam. It meant more work for her, but Amanda was here to work.

She didn't avoid Mokoto, but her gaze grazed past his eyes. She heard two boys laughing as she wrote on the chalkboard. She quickly got out of the classroom, only to enter a heated discussion among the teachers in the staff room.

Mampho had papers strewn on their desk. Figures, rows and columns of numbers. Checks, bills, scholarship forms.

"What's going on?" Amanda asked after Lereko had finished yelling, and he tore a paper out of Mampho's hands.

"Sit," Mothepu commanded. "There's a problem."

Mampho handed Amanda some of the papers. "Look here, Madam Amanda. Madam Phalatsi, she's been stealing money.

Not only had Madam Phalatsi been stealing from the sponsors of orphan students, but she had failed to pay the Ministry of Education the exam fees for the Form Cs and instead had kept the money for herself.

"But if we can't pay these fees, then what?"

Lereko burst out, "Then the Form Cs can't take their exams."

Each student had already paid a large sum of money to the school for exam fees.

The Ministry showed no mercy.

"Where is Madam Phalatsi?"

Mothepu shrugged. "Gone."

The next morning Mokoto was on Amanda's taxi. Amanda sat by Mampho who didn't talk much. They wouldn't have been able to hear each other over the music anyway. But by sitting near Mampho, Amanda felt like she had a friend.

It took over two hours to get into the camptown. Mokoto sat behind her, and his knees pressed into the back of the thin seat. Halfway through the ride Mokoto leaned against Amanda's seat. He rested his head on the seat back. She felt his warmth, and the end of her ponytail got caught between the seat and the crown of his head. She didn't pull away but sat still–still and straight and breathless.

When the taxi got to town, Amanda quickly got off and didn't turn around to acknowledge him. She did her errands. ATM for her monthly stipend, the Chinese shop–a smaller, less commercial version of Wal-Mart– which sold shoes and bread and plastic tubs. Amanda bought sour green apples, rice, canned beans, sardines, a chocolate bar, and an aerosol can of Doom to keep out the ants. She mailed letters home, waiting fifteen minutes for the postal woman to get done with her lunch and sell her stamps. She bought a block of cheese from the butcher. She met another volunteer, Brian, for Maluti beer and chips at the local hotel–a wooden, poorly lit monstrosity beside a primary school.

Amanda told Brian about the beatings.

He shook his head. "My school is even worse." He taught at the large high school in the camptown with over 600 students. "The male teachers make the boys pull down their pants, bend over, and then beat them with a stick. I had a Form C who couldn't even sit down the next day. He bled through his pants." Brian kept on eating, and Amanda knew he had begun to accept it.

The last taxi to Ha Lithaba left between three and four depending on the season, the day, whether or not the taxi got full. Amanda arrived at the taxi rank early, but there were only two seats left. The other woman who wanted to get on the taxi paid before Amanda but pushed Amanda in front of her. She pushed Amanda towards the back—the undesirable taxi seat—where they managed to cram four people together. Amanda shimmied into the back; her bags knocked against the arms of the seated passengers.

Two men made room for her—no one would give up the window seat—and Amanda fit in. She had to sit up a bit, one bag on her feet, the other on her lap, her arms pressed into her sides. The shoulders of the men dug into her ribs as they took up more room.

"Hello, Madam."

Amanda finally noticed Mokoto seated next to her.

"Oh, Mokoto." She blushed. "Hi, how are you?"

His slow smile curled up to his lazy eyelids. The

whites of his eyes glowed around his dark pupils. "I'm fine. How are you?" He couldn't break himself of the habit of structured, polite responses.

The man on Amanda's other side started speaking to Mokoto in Sesotho. The man touched Amanda's hair. The light color attracted curious fingers, but she elbowed him anyway.

"I love you," the man breathed in her ear.

"*Ntate*, be quiet."

He laughed. He had chipped front teeth and drunk-red eyes. "I want to marry you."

"No."

She turned away from him, facing Mokoto. Mokoto spoke quietly to the man. Amanda understood snippets of their conversation: teacher, America, beautiful. Beautiful came from the man, but Mokoto agreed. Or maybe Amanda only imagined that he agreed.

The man got louder, laughing and stroking her hair. The rest of the taxi talked all at once, drowned out by the obnoxiously loud thumping of Basotho music that shook from the speakers. The man breathed beer breaths onto the side of her face.

"I love you." He reached his hand between her legs. Amanda jerked and let go of her bag to slap the man's hands away.

"Stop!"

People twisted around to look at them. Mokoto said something to appease the other passengers. They turned back around, shaking their heads.

"*Ntate!*" Mokoto yelled to the man. His face was stern, but in true, confusing Basotho fashion, he laughed and eased the man back into a blissful, drunken state.

Mokoto leaned over Amanda. "It's okay, Madam."

She smiled. "Thanks, Mokoto."

He watched her. Gently, he slid his hand across hers. She looked forward but didn't move it. His thumb covered her thumb, and he left it there for the rest of the ride.

It was after six when they returned to Ha Lithaba, and the sun had dipped behind the mountains. Only a shimmer of white light fanned out around the peaks.

"*Lekhua!* White woman," the man called, following Amanda out of the taxi. Her hut was a fifteen-minute walk down the road, so she walked quickly.

"Madam." Mokoto jogged up beside her. "It's dark. I will walk with you?"

"Thanks."

The man's voice faded as he gave up the chase.

"Madam, did that man hurt you?"

"No, Mokoto." Amanda was slightly surprised—and pleased—that when he was with her, he looked at her. He listened. Even if he didn't understand, he listened. "Sometimes I get tired—sad—that people touch me and ask me things and laugh at me."

"No, Madam," he said emphatically. "They don't

laugh at you."

They reached Amanda's hut, and as she unlocked the door, Mokoto asked for a glass of water.

The sun was almost gone, so she dumped her bags and lit a candle. Mokoto sat down patiently at the table. Amanda dipped a cup into her bucket of water, feeling bad that she reserved her boiled, filtered water only for herself. He gulped it down and watched her over the rim of the glass as she unpacked her groceries.

"How was your weekend?"

He smiled. "Fine." He corrected himself as Amanda raised her eyebrows. "Marvelous, Madam."

They laughed together. Amanda had spent months breaking her students from the habit of using fine and nice as their only adjectives.

"How was your weekend, Madam?"

So she told him. About her day, about her job, her life. Sometimes he asked questions or answered them, but mostly he just listened.

What did Amanda like about him? Their language was limited. His dreams were limited.

"I want to be a taxi driver," he told her. It made sense; taxi drivers exchanged money, wore flashy clothes and could drive. The complete package for Basotho youth.

So what did she like about him?

"You're beautiful, Madam. And clever."

His honesty. His direct, unabashed gaze. And he

made her skin burn. Amanda remembered his touch from yesterday and the taxi ride today.

"Thank you."

He stood up and touched her cheek, almost reading her mind, her blush.

"Mokoto, stop."

He took both of her hands. He held them at his sides. "Why?"

"In another time, at another moment, this could be right. But we can't—"

"We can."

"We shouldn't."

"Can. Should. You are the English teacher."

"Yes, and this is wrong. You're my student."

"Yes. And a man."

"But—"

"I am a man and you are a woman. It is not wrong."

"It is, Mokoto." She pulled her hands away.

"Why? God is love and God is good. I love you, Madam. That is good."

Amanda knew that love and like were the same word in Sesotho. But something about the way he said it made her think he meant love. He leaned down and kissed her. It was a dry, hot kiss. His mouth hovered over hers. He held her hands again. His touch—warm and dry. His fingertips—soft pads on her hand. She didn't want him to let go.

He wrapped his arms around her. The sky darkened.

"You better go home."

"No," he murmured. "My aunt thinks I am in town."

They lay in her bed, entwined, fully clothed, keeping each other warm. They kissed and talked. And kissed.

"Be with me," he asked.

"I am with you."

"Forever."

She brushed his forehead with her fingers. "Forever doesn't exist. Just this. Just now. And I am with you now." She kissed his confused lips.

"Amanda?" It was the first time he had called her by her name, and she liked the sound of it.

"Yes?"

"Will you stay in Lesotho forever?" He kissed her hand.

"Oh, Mokoto. My home is in America."

"But Ha Lithaba is your home too."

"I suppose. Will you stay here forever?"

"No." His eyes darkened. "I hate the village. I hate the school." He gripped her hand tightly.

"Why do you hate the school? You don't hate me."

His chest pulsated. "No. I love you. But the teachers are bad. Madam Phalatsi is cruel. They hate us, Amanda."

"No, they don't."

"Yes. They beat us. They do not let us eat."

"Mokoto."

"The students are angry. And we know about the

money."

Amanda sat up. "What money?"

Mokoto gleamed in the dark as he looked up at Amanda. "The Form Cs' exam money. We know it's gone."

"How?"

"The village talks. If I can't take the exam, I can't come back next year. It is too expensive."

"I'm sorry."

"We will stop them, Amanda."

"Shh." She touched his lips. He reached up for her hair that fell around her shoulders. They were creating a story she would not share with her fellow volunteers, with her friends back home. She leaned into him and did not think of them.

In the early hours he left. The rest of the weekend Amanda stayed indoors, afraid that the village would talk. But Mokoto kept them a secret. Days passed. She went to school and avoided Mokoto's stares. But outside of school, in the early evenings, they saw each other. They had fleeting moments—whispers of moments. There was no dawn—only night and day. Night stalked fast. Then he would be gone.

Mokoto pulled her aside after assembly one day, behind the staff room. Amanda had just been speaking with Mampho. Word was going around in the village that Madam Phalatsi had arrived in a private taxi the night before. To pack her things and move out. "Family death," Mampho said skeptically. Madam Phalatsi hadn't come to school though.

Mokoto touched her wrist. "I want to marry you."

"No."

"Why?"

She took his hands. "In ten months I'm leaving. To go back to America. This—us—is going to end."

"Take me with you."

She sighed. "I can't."

"Why?"

"I've got to be on my own. And so do you. You're going to finish school and get a job and have a good life. But you're going to do it in Lesotho, just as I have to do it in America."

He frowned. "You need to leave."

"What?" Amanda pulled back.

"Don't come to school tomorrow."

"Mokoto, I don't understand what you're saying. It's my job to be here."

He leaned in. She smelled his hot breath and the dirty sheep-smell of his sweater. "Please promise, Amanda, that you won't come to school."

They heard the rustle of the teachers leaving the staff room. "Fine," she said hurriedly. "I won't come." Amanda thought he was going to kiss her, but he turned quickly and ran down into the ravine.

She thought about not going to school. But when

morning puffed through her windows, Amanda rose and dressed and left for school, just as she did every day. She was determined that everything would go back to normal with Mokoto. She would stay his teacher and nothing more. When exams ended he would no longer be at her school, would no longer be her student. It was clear yesterday that he was mad at her.

A clamorous mix of voices came from the classrooms. Amanda assumed it was another day where no one would teach, but instead of going in and reprimanding the students, she headed straight for the staff room. She would put off seeing Mokoto as long as possible.

The staff room door was locked. Mampho banged on the only window, which had become permanently stuck a month ago. "Help, Amanda," she cried. "The students have locked us in." Nthibeleng, who was in charge of the keys for the kitchen, had stolen the staff room keys. And the doors locked from the outside with a padlock.

Amanda turned to face the classrooms. She could see a crowd of students in the Form C classroom. They began chanting, screaming, wailing like a mass of crazed singers. She went to the door which was locked too. She banged on it.

"Let me in!"

Students pushed and shoved, but Mokoto made his way to the door and opened up. The students shrieked louder. Little Nthibeleng clapped her hands, fingers widespread.

Mokoto wedged himself in the doorway between Amanda and the classroom. She saw a crowd of kids with sticks and their metal lunch bowls, banging them together.

Mokoto grabbed her shoulders. "Leave, Amanda. I told you to leave."

"What are you doing?" she cried.

His beautiful face was broken with anger. "I said that I would stop them. We are not animals. We are not stupid."

"No. You aren't." She clung to him, and then saw over his shoulder the crumpled body of Madam Phalatsi on the floor. A boy went up to her and kicked her in the face.

"Stop!" Amanda started crying. "Leave her alone!" The boy turned around and glared at her.

"Amanda." Mokoto stroked her face. "You must run." He pushed her away from him. "I love you. But run."

Amanda ran. The sounds of screaming got lost in the mountains, but the beautiful blackness of Mokoto's face stayed with her. She remembered his face and ran.

Alice's Bedfellow

Alice slept with a shotgun on her lap. She'd curl up on the couch, with a blanket around her shoulders, the gun straddled along her middle, the barrel pointed towards the floor. The gun dull and long. The floor sallow and expectant.

She slept like this five nights out of the week when her husband Marcus delivered pizzas in Nelspruit, twenty kilometers away. They lived on a farm. A dry, whittled away farm under a pale South African sky.

Alice would wait for Marcus in her sleep. She slept lightly not only to awaken at the sound of his footsteps but to be alert for what might visit her during the night.

During the day, the farm was quiet. The cows roamed in the spaces between the fields. An old uncle or auntie might walk along the road but only with a destination in mind—the city, the market, the taxi junction. Rarely did anyone look at the farmhouse—a small, white wooden edifice built in haste and left to whither with the crops.

But the night was different. The shadows roamed at night. Strips of the night sky shredded apart and manifested into burglars, murderers and rapists in Alice's mind.

It began seven months ago when Alice had forgotten the sheets drying on the line. She made it out onto the veranda when she heard a grunt in the trees at the edge of the house's property.

"Who's there?" she had called, nearly tripping down the steps.

Silence responded.

The next day she had read in the paper that nine chickens had gone missing from a farm ten kilometers away.

"Probably foxes," Marcus had said.

Alice pointed to the paper. "The coop was cut with a wire cutter. Foxes aren't precise."

"Most people aren't either." And Marcus had chuckled at his own joke.

But the next night he loaded the shotgun and showed Alice how to aim and shoot.

Marcus wasn't stupid. He kept a switchblade in his uniform pocket. Pizzas weren't a valuable commodity, but his delivery truck certainly was.

He was a bit concerned that Mina would get too close to the gun.

Mina was barely two, with round cheeks and light-brown hair. She could walk. She could touch Alice in the night and scare her, and the gun could accidentally go off. She could—

"Stop it Marcus. I'm already worried."

Marcus touched Alice's shoulder. She was a large woman–more suited for wrestling cattle than Marcus was. Her neck was soft and thick, and Marcus leaned over and kissed the pillow of flesh at the base of her neck where it met her broad shoulder. Marcus adored Alice's concern.

"We'll shut her door and put the baby gate up. She'll be fine."

Marcus had lived near Nelspruit his whole life, and his only "encounter" with a black person had been when two black teenagers had cornered him in Jo'Burg—not even in Nelspruit—and asked for his money. He had given them the fifty rand he always kept in his coat pocket—a pacifier for potential muggers. He stored his wallet under his shirt in a pouch like travelers used.

Alice was from Pretoria. She had seen black people from the safety of her house.

"Guards protected me," she had told Marcus once, when he asked her if she had been scared her whole life.

"Yes," he said slowly, over coffee, "but who guards the guards?"

So on a cold night in July—July the middle of winter—Alice slept by the electric heater. The heater buzzed. Outside, a calculated rattle of chains. Alice jolted awake. Her eyes two deep buckets, the color lost amidst her pupils. The shotgun had slept between her sweaty hands and was now clammy.

She held her breath and listened.

A deliberate creak trying to be silent. It reminded Alice of when she was a child trying to sneak out of her room, and the slower she crept, the more the wooden floorboards in her parents' house moaned.

But this was not the noise of someone trying to get out, but someone–somewhere–trying to get in.

She pressed her arms near her sides and strained her neck in the act of close listening. There was no wind. A cow mooed. A step on the veranda squeaked.

Alice got up. "Get out of here. I have a gun."

Alice thought about those horrible American movies that Marcus was addicted to. Always showing women creeping about, panicky, only to be ambushed from behind, never prepared. Barely thinking, Alice raised the gun and rushed towards the front door.

"Aah!" She yelled loud enough in the house, a piddle in the empty night. She banged open the door still howling. She stomped on the porch. She raised the gun and shot towards a star. The boom thrust Alice back. Alice thought her hearing might be gone. Then she heard Mina screaming upstairs.

"Next time I'll kill you," she shouted.

The night soaked up her threat.

Alice went back inside. She locked the door, turned on every light and prepared some milk for Mina.

Over cold chicken pizza, Alice told Marcus what happened.

"You're a brave woman," he said, squeezing her chubby hand. Alice had child's hands, with deep dimples and silky palms. "If they know what's good for them, they won't come back."

"I don't think you should work at nights anymore, Marcus."

He blotted the grease of his pizza off with a napkin. "That's not practical, and you know it."

"I don't like being alone."

"I'll get us another dog." They had a dog once, but a year ago it got hit by a tourist's SUV and bled to death on the side of the road.

"Every time it barked, I'd be nervous."

"It would be a deterrent."

Alice fed Mina bits of chicken. "A dog can be killed just as easily as a person."

They already had bars on the first floor windows. So Marcus bought a second lock for the front door. Alice didn't care about locks.

"There's no one out here to hear me screaming. A burglar could have all night to get inside."

Alice once saw a man beaten to death in Pretoria. It was a black beating a black. "But if that's what they do to their own, think of what they would do to one of us."

Apartheid ended fifteen years before, but Alice had a hard time forgetting. "Think of how we treated them, Marcus. Would you forgive us?"

"I didn't do anything to them."

She whispered so Mina couldn't hear. "You say *kaffir*."

"I also called my mother a bitch, but she got over it."

Marcus donned his pizza hat and shirt at 8:00. He kissed Mina on her sleepy brow, patted Alice's butt. He got in the truck and drove off to Nelspruit by 8:15. Once he left, Alice locked both locks and got the gun.

She hoisted Mina against her chest, the gun clutched in her free hand. She put Mina to bed. Baby burps and wishy-washy dreams floated in the nursery.

The wind spoke that night. Whispered against the windowpanes. Murmured at the veranda steps. Licked up against the house.

Alice took up her place on the couch, near the front door. She tried to watch the TV, but every show was splotched with gun noises and bangs and screams.

Alice wasn't much of a reader, but she tried to skim a newspaper article. "Rape in the Park." Not a story to lift her spirits. She tore up the story and left the shreds on the coffee table—which wasn't really a table but an old trunk, flat on top with brass buckles. It had belonged to Alice's father and was given to her and Marcus on their wedding day. Alice's father used to keep his valuables in the trunk— because the trunk had been too heavy for one man to move and too locked up to get broken into. She kept linen in there now.

The next story she attempted to read was about a bomb threat. The next: "Speaker Murdered." "Foetus Found in Alley." "Woman Attacked." Each story she tore up until the pile of shredded paper on the trunk looked like the bottom of a hamster's cage.

The rest of the paper was filled with classifieds, for jobs she wasn't qualified for and ads for things she and Marcus couldn't afford to purchase. New cars. Used cars. Cosmetics. Exotic birds. A fish tank. A refurbished computer. There were blurbs about politicians too corrupt. Too idiotic. Too unconcerned.

Alice felt like crying, but she wasn't much of a crier.

The last time she had cried was Mina's birth. She held Mina, pink and sleeping–her head soft and fleshy like a peach, resting in her palm. She had cried because peaches were so easily smashed in this world. And Alice had felt more helpless than her newborn. She had wanted to stuff Mina back in her womb and keep her warm and safe forever.

Alice fell asleep with tears in her eyes.

Outdoors the wind sang a lullaby. Of hidden crevices and fallen leaves. Of broken twigs and covered footsteps.

It could've been the wind that woke Alice up. The grandfather clock pointed to 11:27. There were noises from outside. Alice couldn't tell if they were night noises or farm noises. Or intruder noises.

The lights were off.

She opened the window slightly to listen. There was a distinct rustling sound. Movement in the yard. The bushes moved twice–once with the wind, once by an unseen force.

Alice opened the front door. She unlocked each lock slowly. She shimmied out between the small gap created by the open door. Now she could see the bushes breathing. The bushes waited, knowing she was there.

Alice was too frightened to shout. She imagined a large black man with a silver knife. Her screaming couldn't stop an attack.

She aimed the barrel of the gun at the bushes, and remembering what Marcus had shown her, she rested the gun into the nook of her shoulder–steady–and pulled the trigger.

The blast shimmered in her ears and then went out like a candle flame. There was a guttural groan, a jerk in the bushes.

"Shit." She backed up into the house and relocked the door. "Shit, shit, shit." She set the gun on the ground and curled up in front of the door. She waited, her breath raspy.

The gun lay unassuming on the floor. There was only wind outside.

When Marcus returned, he came in through the back door and flicked on the living room light. He found Alice pale and huddled by the door. "Alice? Jesus, what's wrong?" He approached her slowly.

He saw the gun–alone–on the floor. He searched for Mina, looked for blood.

"Where's Mina?"

"Asleep."

Marcus exhaled deeply. He crouched down. His knees creaked with stiffness. He placed his hands on Alice's shoulders. "What happened?"

Her large face quivered. Her cheeks melted into her jawline. "I shot someone."

"Where? Who?" He gripped her shoulders tighter to punctuate his questions (where—*grip*—who—*grip*).

"On the veranda."

Marcus looked beyond Alice—at the door—perhaps anticipating that the dead body (if there really was a body) would come knocking.

"Are you sure?"

"I don't know."

"Move away from the door."

Alice needed to be told what to do. She nodded and crawled to the center of the room. Marcus picked up the gun. Alice moaned slightly. He opened the door. Marcus shoved the barrel of the gun into the bushes, swinging it back and forth. "Oh, Christ." The *thwack* of branches and shimmying fabric of leaves but also a *phwip* of hitting a soft solidness. Like a bag of feed. Like a human stomach.

"Hello?" Marcus called, clueless about what else to say. "Get me a light." But Alice wouldn't move.

He shuffled back towards the door, reached his right arm inside to find the veranda light. It was a bare bulb, and somehow the shadows were blacker next to the new spread of light. Marcus, gun in hand, pushed his other hand into the bushes. The body was small and thin, and in the forgiving light he saw a boy's face.

Age was a fickle determiner–and Marcus thought of all the dead people he had seen (his mother, his brother Leonard, his childhood friend, shot in the chest) and how innocent they looked–how young they appeared in death. Not unlike Mina when she slept. Or Alice, for that matter, on those rare nights when Marcus caught her asleep, before she woke up to greet him home.

So this could be a ten-year-old just as easily as a fifteen-year-old. But he was a boy. And black. And dead. Strangely warm (not of life, but of cooling meat). He wore a brown t-shirt, torn, where a defined shoulder poked through. His clothes were dirty, but his skin was scrubbed clean. Maybe he had a mother somewhere who pecked at him to bathe. Maybe he was stealing for her.

Or, even more likely, maybe he was an orphan, fending for himself. Or maybe–and Marcus felt guilty thinking of it–he was trying to just sleep.

Then he saw the knife looped through a chain on the boy's pants.

"Marcus?" Alice had crawled to the doorway, sitting up against the door, her head resting back, her chin raised and mouth opened, as though waiting to catch raindrops.

"It's a boy."

"Oh, God." She sucked in air like a beached fish.

The boy was crumpled. The bullet had gone through his head. The back of his head, bloody, brainy. Alice gagged.

"We need to bury him."

Alice only nodded.

"Get a shovel."

There was a shovel in the barn. Alice got a flashlight. Marcus felt the damp soil beneath the bushes. There was a smoothed out dip where the boy had been huddled.

The yard was dry. The fields rocky. The bushes alive and damp. Alice brought back the shovel, deposited it at Marcus' feet and scurried to the veranda. She crouched in the living room light, a sanctuary.

Marcus dug under the bushes, breaking branches, scattering leaves, upturning ground stained with the boy's blood.

"Get me a blanket."

There was a quilt stored in the trunk, so Alice got it. It smelled musty, of old clothes and stale furniture. Of unturned book pages and dust. Alice handed it to Marcus.

He had dug a narrow, deep hole. The earth kept falling in and he would–*Fuck*–and then scoop it back out. He tried not to look at the boy's head.

Alice couldn't stop looking at his head. She couldn't not imagine that she was now a murderer. She turned away and threw up on the veranda steps.

Marcus wrapped the quilt around the boy. He gently rolled the quilted boy into the hole. As Alice heaved and cried, Marcus packed dirt on top of the boy's body.

"We should say something. That's what his mother would want," Alice sniffed.

"Okay." Marcus sat back on his heels, Alice kneeled on the veranda. They bowed their heads. Alice kept crying.

Marcus noticed that his hands were shaking. He buried a dead body, and only now could he feel sick and scared.

He didn't believe in God. He didn't *not* believe in him either. He clutched his hands to both stop the shaking and to pray. Or something like it.

"God," the word was tricky on his lips, "please take care of this boy. May he rest in peace." Marcus cleared his throat and thought of funerals he had attended. Of families and friends. How this boy was alone under the bushes.

"I'm sorry," burst Alice, and she sobbed, her child-like hands barely covering her wide, wet face. "Oh, God, I'm sorry."

In the morning, Alice cooked eggs but didn't eat them. Marcus left early to feed the cows. Mina threw bits of egg on the floor, but Alice didn't pick them up. She stared at the front door and thought she heard the bushes breathing.

Ausi With No Name

They eat by paraffin lamp. The light is intense but small, giving off enough heat to make sweat on their upper lips, the saltiness of it mixing with their food.

They do not really see what they eat but rather the shadows of the sugar bowl and the chicken wings, giving an illusion to the actual shapes. If it weren't for the heavy coat of cooking oil on everything, it would be like eating shadows.

In the daytime she's a shadow—following the others around, cleaning up after them. She is dark—but not any darker than the rest of them, except that her heart is black.

She has a bastard child.

His name is Thato. She has lost her own name and is now—simply—Mathato. She is Thato's mother.

When Thato is grown and she is sick, hunched over in wasting pain, she will think back to before he was born and try desperately to remember her name. Whether from illness or suppression, she won't be able to.

She remembers now, of course, for Thato is not quite two. Though she doesn't see the point in trying to remember it because that girl is gone.

***

She got her hair done up today.

A weave braided into her stubby mess, pulled so tight the corners of her eyes have puckered up. She might be crying at any moment.

It is nearing Christmas. A tender, food-rich day stuffed in a summer month. In Lesotho, Christmas is not of snow and presents and really not so much about the Christ Child but about sunshine and heat and food and a new hairdo. It's about looking good in a new dress and hiding the sweat beneath the fabric–tucking the heat in the folds of your body–and letting it escape at night, after the feasting and the dancing, when you plunge into a cool bath.

Mathato bathes in the kitchen. Her kitchen is her bedroom is her bathroom is her parlor. She lives in a one-room rondavel, tucked behind the house of her parents, neighboring the sheep pen. In the Basotho culture, one room has many parts. An invisible line separates private quarters from public ones. Any 'me, or woman, can walk in and within a second's glance determine whether your invisible line has been properly drawn.

Mathato places her basin under the kitchen window–low enough so that no one can peek in–but still able to feel the morning sun on her back–the dry air drying her as she washes.

She washes twice a day because the dust blows beneath the door crack, settles on her sticky skin. She likes to be clean–and cleaning is really the only thing she has.

She heats water first. The day before she hauled water–buckets and buckets of it–propped up in her rusty wheelbarrow. The pump is down the lane–a half-kilometer from her house. The local children play there, leaning up against the pump, kicking bare feet in the wet dirt. Their over-sized shirts, torn at the neck, hang off their shoulders. Christmas clothes are tucked away in bo-'me rooms–sharp and soft–with the tags still on.

The older ones–the ones who attend the secondary school in the vale–slit their eyes and whisper to each other behind the backs of their hands. There was a day when a tall boy, sporting a bucket hat, tilted on the back of his head, wrinkled his lips at her, and then spit at her when she turned away.

Her body is not her own anymore but the body of her family–her house. Her sex is not private but judged–gawked at–leered at.

She is the only one to get water.

Ntate tucks straw into the donkey's stall, while 'Me sweeps. The braying donkey and the swish of the broom are the only voices that speak to her in the morning.

The village bo-'me waft into the yard. They step on the heels of their shoes, cracked soles and dusted toes, shuffling into the yard. They are in the shape of ntate canes–their heads tipping at the ends of their necks, looking at their feet. They are ragbags–layers of shirts and dresses, tall boots, and wool blankets wrapped around their waists, sitting on their buttocks, tied underneath their sagging breasts. They wear the same thing year-round. 'Me wears a fedora; the others wear scarves or snow caps.

In the mornings they talk about their children–how the papa burned yesterday (due to the faulty fire or absent-minded daughter–for they never neglect their domestic duties)–how hot it is or who is pregnant or sleeping with whose husband. They speak it quickly then it's off to the water pump or the bus or the shop.

Mathato isn't allowed to sit with them. She is neither 'me nor ausi.

She takes over the sweeping and sweeps around their feet.

"Go feed the chickens," 'Me says though she has already done so. The bo-'me jut their bottom lips out and stare at her with watery eyes. So she walks out to the chicken coop, which is behind the pit latrine. She squats by the coop and counts her knuckles. She rubs her left hand–smoothing the skin that starts to prune, where the black surface meets the pink. She counts the knuckles: 1…2…3…4...5…12345–tapping each with an index finger. She does that five times and returns to the yard.

"I'm going into the city with 'Me Maneo."

That's all 'Me says. She refuses to tell Mathato when she will return. Mathato will do the daily chores–make the bread, wash the clothes, mop the floors.

Ntate and her herd brothers take the sheep to the veld, leaving her by herself. And, of course, there's Thato.

Thato wears a shirt and no nappy. There's a strand of beads around his light brown middle–to ward off the devil and bad luck. His uncircumcised penis dangles beneath. Thato walks around unsupervised. When Mathato cares, she takes an old robe belt and ties it loosely around Thato's neck, holding onto the lengthier end like a leash.

This day–the day before Christmas–a man comes into the yard. The chickens squawk and disperse from the front stoop as he walks amongst them. Thato screeches in baby lingo and Mathato comes to the kitchen door. She stands with her hands resting on the doorway, her bare feet shift back and forth.

She waits for him to speak.

"Lumela," he says–his voice thick like the grass on the mountains.

"Hello." She doesn't smile.

"How are you?" His voice over-enunciates each word–draws out the vowel sounds.

"Fine." She doesn't really know if she's fine or not. Fine is a filter word–an answer–a conversation that she rarely has.

"You *are* fine."

"What do you want?"

He smiles, his sharp yellow teeth glow in a dark brown face. "You always ask questions you have the answers to. I like that about you."

She wants to say no, but she steps aside, and he comes

in. There's no one around her anyway—no one to help, but no one to judge.

Her house is but one room. From the bed they move to the table.

Her skin—clay-wet beneath his body—is dry and cold in the light of the paraffin lamp. After dinner she fixes a cup of coffee. She takes her routine two scoops of creamer, three spoonfuls of sugar. She stirs it then sips a spoonful, testing the taste, warmth. She slurps it and taps her spoon against her plate. The drops of milky coffee are like her tears—brown and few.

The man thought she would cry beneath him. But her eyes fixed above, not at the sky, but at the room corners, blank and still, her jaw slack. It is the look she gets when her baby suckles, when she kneads bread, when she sits in church. The only time she did not have this gaze was during childbirth. Her eyes were squeezed shut then—so maybe that gaze was behind those squeezed eyes too.

And of course there was that one other time.

It is getting late. He puts some money on the table. Her body slopes in the chair. The man watches her. He notices that her ankles and wrists are slight—her shoulders narrow and her arms are plump with muscle and fat. Her collarbone peeks from underneath her smooth skin. She has strong fingers and a wide nose with a round end. Her lips are fleshy, and her chocolate eyes glance around the room, lifting beneath eyelids from time to time.

A moth shimmers into the room, and she follows it

with a raised head. Her lips purse–like this is the most interesting moment in her life.

But it isn't.

***

Men are not allowed. They scatter like chickens to the bar, soaking up bottles of joala, forgetting that they don't have jobs and that another baby is being born into this world.

"We die quicker than we're being born," says one man, short and grey, his black eyes lost in his face.

"Yes, but it doesn't change the fact that there's no food anyway. We'll need to die quicker to feed all of the children," says another, hidden beneath a green blanket and cowboy hat.

Then they forget why they are there and keep on drinking.

The village women bring the water. They balance buckets on their heads. With age and grace they do not spill a drop. They do this every day, but today they do not speak words. Their eyes meet and blink rapidly, and they follow one another to the stone house. Candles are lit in the windows, though it is not quite dusk. The milky-purple sky still gives off light, and the moon is a pale, afternoon crescent, undetected amidst the clouds. The far off mountains groan with thunder. This baby will be born in a storm.

Inside, the house is brown with quickening darkness.

The ausi lies on the floor–on mats and blankets and thin towels. Tonight, once it's over, they will be washed and used as rags. Nothing gets thrown out.

She grits her teeth, and an old 'me sticks a folded up strip of cloth between them, so she doesn't bite her tongue. She's like a horse with its bit.

She snorts and sweats, and her bare feet slip on the floor. Two old women each take a foot, clamping it down with their hands. They move automatically, the strain in their tendons and the whites of their fingernails giving indication of the pressure it takes to hold a birthing woman down.

Ausi does not scream, but her eyes roll back, and her neck throbs, and from the darkness between her legs, a head struggles. It is sticky and black and shaped like a bloated squash–oblong and full. It screams. It is alive. And covered in her blood.

The bo-'me hold it up in the candlelight. Lightning flashes–illuminating its grotesque face.

The ausi faints.

***

Her stomach is a hard, round ball, and her buttocks balance it–soft and firm with days of papa meals and bread to fatten her up.

She doesn't sit now for fear that she won't be able to get up. She leans against walls or rests her hands on tabletops and bends over, as if in prayer or illness, then heavily stands back up, her left fingertips touching the crease in her back, her right palm cupping her stomach.

Her ankles and toes are swollen, and she goes around barefoot. Her toenails are chipped from dirt and rocks. At night, before she goes to sleep, she soaks them in salt water. It is the only time she sits.

It is hot. Rather, she is hot, but she does not sweat. Only the palms of her hands get clammy. Her feet and neck and throat are dry. She wears a wool plaid blanket tied around her waist, right below her breasts. She doesn't wear the blanket to cover up or to hide.

Everyone already knows–though it's wrong to ask. Bad luck and the baby could die. It could die anyway, but she doesn't think that.

No, she wears the blanket out of maternal instinct. She's already trying to protect it. To keep it warm in this dry-ice world.

She wants a little girl, so she can dress her in skirts and tie bows in her hair and kiss her soft, red lips and name her Lintle–Beautiful. But she knows it is much harder for a girl.

So she prays for a boy.

***

The clinic is one room. It sits back from the road, creeping in the dip of the valley. It has a red roof and two small windows. It lets in sunlight from the north, so it is only open until three. One day out of the month a medical staff comes to monitor pregnant women and to test for HIV. It's a government service.

The ausi stands because there are no chairs. She would sit outside, under the aloe trees, but she doesn't want anyone to see her.

She wears her good dress today–red with white stripes–and a black and gold blazer with large gold buttons. She wears a thin gold bracelet on her right wrist. He gave it to her as a present, and every so often she touches it. The other women in the clinic eye her bracelet. She knows they are jealous–or curious–or both– and that makes the corners of her mouth twitch. She doesn't smile often.

She has already had the test. Waiting is the hardest part. They were safe–he was gentle–the test is probably needless, but she feels comfortable and mature. He asked her to come–to make sure. Only someone truly in love would ask that.

A nurse motions to the ausi. They go into the far corner (there are no walls, just a thin curtain) and sit down in two plastic chairs.

The nurse tries out a smile then looks down at the chart.

"I'm not sure if congratulations are in order or not. It depends on the circumstances. Is there…a man in the picture?"

"That's why I'm here."

"Ok. Well, it's positive."

The ausi's knees jerk. "How could that be something to congratulate me for?"

"I just thought."

"What? That," she lowers her voice, "that HIV is some kind of rite—some sort of prize for giving yourself to a man no one trusts. Huh?"

She counts her knuckles, trying to breathe. Is it possible she can talk without breathing?

"Oh." The nurse touches her tapping knuckles. "No, I don't mean HIV." She spits the letters out. "I mean the pregnancy test. You're going to have a baby."

"What?" Now it is Ausi who is stunned. "But I didn't take that test."

The nurse ruffles through her papers. She holds up two, clarifies that she has the ausi's name correct. Apparently, they did both tests.

"And you are pregnant," the nurse reaffirms, as though doubting her own authority.

"And the other test?" Ausi sits up straighter, all at once conscious that there's something inside her. That she could be crushing it, by slouching and folding her stomach.

The nurse looks at the second piece of paper. Her eyes flicker and go out. Without looking at the ausi she nods her head.

She keeps tapping her knuckles, but with one quick cry, she starts to breathe.

***

She swooshes onto his bed as though she's a frequent visitor—as though her round figure knows every dip and hollow of its mattress.

But she isn't. This is the first time she has been to his place.

They've spent months together, but always at discotheques or jazz bars (the saxophones shrill, their notes clanging against her gin and tonics) or quiet, dark restaurants in Pietermaritzburg or even Durban. She's been there once–with him. He fed her exotic Indian food with his fingers. Basotho always eat with their hands but not white men. They use forks and spoons and knives. He fed her, though, because he said that's what lovers do. Lover. The word makes her spine hot, like a mountain flash of lightning.

He has never been to her house.

She always meets him in a taxi or in a hotel lobby– where it is crowded and safe. She has never been to his house. Until now. This is only one of several, he informs her. He has a large home in Pretoria. This little house is for business because he works so much in her country.

She lounges on his bed. It is soft and deep and smells like him–thick and warm and pungent. She has dropped her high heels by the door. Her bare feet–recently softened and soaped–tap against the bed frame. She smiles but keeps it low, so it flutters near her chest.

He stands by the dresser and loosens his collar. She sees her reflection in the mirror behind him, and for a moment tilts her head, flutters her lashes, and slides her tongue across her teeth. She seduces him, but really she is seducing herself. Finally, she catches his eye.

"Are you comfortable?" he asks.

"I'm a bit hot." She touches the edge of her dress.

"We can fix that," he says, coming to her.

She's been close to him before—has danced in his arms, kissed his chin, his neck, his mouth. But this closeness is different. He stands over her, and she wants him to lie down, or she wants to stand up. He crawls onto the bed.

He is all heat, and the room feels even hotter now. Not blaring summertime-sun heat or sweaty-working-all-day heat, but low, being-burned-alive heat, hiding-in-your-mother's-womb heat.

"Are you scared?" he asks.

She shakes her head, but she is.

"I've been with African women before."

She doesn't know how to take that. He was born in Jo'Burg. He is an African.

"Black women," he adds, as though reading her thoughts. "I find black women the most beautiful of all women." His fingertips touch her lips, drawing their plump shape. "And you're the most beautiful of them."

And she has never been called beautiful. As he reaches for her, she cries—out of happiness in love—but out of sadness too. That this may be her last time, as well as her first. But nonetheless a brilliant time, when her eyes are stars and he calls her name.

PART TWO

Employed in Africa

This is a country polluted by white-colored cars. That's all those diplomats and those foreign-fuckers teachers volunteers baithopi drive like they've got somewhere to go in god's sweet cloud-white chariots but I don't give a damn who they are or think they are because what I think they are is the only important matter here. Hear this–I scouted out the place long before you came here. I watched it like a vigilant orphan pup looking for a drop of milk from momma's teat. I could be that man selling oranges in dusty boxes or that one muttering to himself asking for loose change but I got purpose because that's the only thing a person needs to have and I got purpose with any of those white shiny cruisers that swim like sharks out of gates.

Tires are burning today. There's a riot on of stupid people who don't like the election results and burn things because everyone–even the good ones in white cars–can't resist the heat and power of starting fires. So tires burn and people flee. Windows smash and this is when all the good white cars with their tinted windows to keep faces inside blank and unassuming drive out from locks and bars and shut doors to cross the border into some shredded half-masked place of safety. But where there are guns and hungry people there is no safety. And there are always guns. And always hungry people. Unless you live in america but they make guns so there you go.

I choose the corner by the alley near the street called king where one last white toyota land cruiser cruises out– the gate locked behind and he stops like a good beaten-down driver who kisses a lot of ass behind those walls– and stops full-stop. At the stop sign. And I get up knock on his window and hit it with a crowbar and he jumps away from the flying glass in the terror of surprise and I claw his neck with the bar and say move over and he moves out through the passenger door. I get in. He shouts and then I'm off. Just me and my car now–the driver the owner. And I smell rubber and notice that even inside these nice leather seats the air still carries dust because no one escapes the air pollution.

The Taxi Rank

There's a little girl with a teddy bear strapped to her back like a baby–a backpack–a gun–fitted fittingly firmly to her back, slung on with a blanket like her mother used to carry her, baby burps bouncing between the shoulder blades. She is pushed in the crowd of buyers and sellers and gawkers. *Buy me sweets? Buy me an orange? Buy me a knock-off cassette tape of Famu music? And buy me nail clippers so I don't have to use my teeth?* Pink ice creams melt between fingers, eating in a closed off kombi to not breathe in TB which lurks under seats and down throats. The sheep strapped to the roof, and its urine streams down the window like yellow rain. A Dutch tourist sits on my lap and I show off my recently mined Sesotho words. *Rondavel means house* though it's a hacked Afrikaner word. There's an old man scooped like a question mark due to the sack of oranges he totes on his back. He sells them for five cents more than he bought them, and this is called a profit. I pay the conductor in bills of King Moshoeshoe and lion heads in Easter greens and blues. *Take me to Maseru to Mokhotlong to Ficksburg. Take me away from here.* He charges me more and writes my name down in a book next to my destination–neat and black–the letters little soldiers spelling out the Sesotho name I wear here: Lerato. Love.

A Bottle Full of Nothing

This dagga feels good smoking in smoking out. And bits of smoke ride in front of my eyes and out...well, out there somewhere. I'm here I pat this nice crate box seat nice cuz it isn't the ground. My back leans up against the wall of the bar. The voices of bottles and men from inside, they rattle through my head.

"Ho joang," Thabo greets me. "Whatcha doing?" He's a blur of black and red walking through the door.

"Nothing," I say, but he's gone, flish-flash cuz my lips move slow.

Each day is winter slow, long dark days of nothing to do but sit and drink. Sitting and drinking cuz there aren't any jobs. Or are there jobs and they just won't take me?

"Thabo!" I shout and he comes out then, twin bottles twinkling in his hands. "How come I don't have a job?"

He laughs. Cuz that's what we all do. Sit and drink and laugh. "The mine closed. No more diamonds."

"No mines huh?" Though can't remember through my wishy-washy brain if I worked there. "South Africa has mines. Lots and lots of mines."

"This isn't South Africa, Bokang. Lesotho is poor, not like South Africa."

"We're poor. Poor poor poor."

That's why there's no food only papa–boiled maize

meal–crumbly like the crumble mountain rocks. Dry cuz there's no rain. No rain, no food. No money, no food. No job, no money. A lot of nothing in Lesotho.

Thabo leaves and others come and go go and come. The sun is too bright–too burning white bright like if smoke was solid it'd be like that and get in your eyes and burn. I hear nothing but cows and laughter and wind–I feel like my head is blown away but my feet are still here, so I must be here. I'm dizzy with nothing to do.

A chicken struts by pecking into the ground and coming up with more nothing. It's ugly-like, scraggly and dust-ruffled. But under dusty feathers I can almost taste fried chicken on my sour tongue. And my wife and children love fried chicken. And we're all hungry and it's right there. And I'm right here.

I take off my blanket wrapped for unneeded warmth and stumble across its path. I pin it down. Squawk squawk squawk. My arms are twisted in the blanket and when I can tell arms from blanket I take my near-empty bottle and drink the rest–glug glug glug–and bonk it over the chicken's head. Dead and done just like that.

I go inside the ugly bar and ask for a plastic sack and another bottle. No money but always drink. No job but always food. The plastic crunch crunch crunches. I pull up the blanket with a swoosh and nothing there. Just one feather and lots of dust. No one around but cows that blur into the rock that blurs into the mountains that blur into the clouds in the sky. One world that's so blurry it looks like nothing.

Circumcise

We will slice away the foreskin and this is how we will save Africa. For don't all rich people want to be saviors? Of the earth and money and opportunities and, occasionally, people? The R.S.A., as a nation, is slacking–on something so mundane as circumcision. The missionaries fucked that up: don't do it, do it. Minds are malleable like rain-softened dirt, and what was once dirty isn't. We all stand in line, dozens of us, droves of us, waiting behind flimsy curtains spread out on tables, thinned, pull-back and healthy. What will it mean for us? To have our penises exposed? Afterwards it is clean, not in the way my home is clean, or my laundry or my skin when I've washed it in soapy suds. It is a different kind of clean. And when I sleep with my woman I feel it in a thousand tiny explosions, like waves popping onto the shores.

Prince Harry Flew Into the Village

He came from away far far. Far far away. I live in a yellow country called Lesotho. And he is three hand-lengths away in a pink country called England, according to the map painted on the classroom wall. I like pink because it doesn't grow in the village. Pink is hidden on tongues and woven in clothes. I can't grab pink, but I can grab green and brown and white.

He came from the clouds. The helicopter fell from the sky to the football field. So we couldn't show him the game I played so well. His skin was white and I could see his veins, like looking through clouds and seeing the sky. And his hair was like river rocks.

We were told not to ask for sweets. We sang songs instead and ran to hug his legs. I touched his waist and my cheek rested on his shirt and it was soft. He had tea with the teachers and I watched through the window. The younger ones sat near the door and listened. He spoke English I couldn't understand.

I gave him a picture I drew of a horse and clouds in the shape of airplanes and a mountain that looked like a pointy hat. He said it was the greatest gift he's ever gotten. (But he looked over my head as he said this. And I knew that he lied.)

Where the Lions Roamed

Between diamond mines and rondavels, lions once sat. They licked their paws and cradled cubs. Lions were hunted for fur and draped as capes across the shoulders of hunters. The King is drawn in history books, wearing a lion like a golden gown. Lions bit princes and tore flesh from their women. They took more from the women because they too were female. Fleas kept company by their ears and flies flirted with their eyelids. They ate the baboons and plucked cows from their herds. But the people were more desperate for the land, and they speared them beyond the borders, through their hearts. They competed for food. And space.

And now lions are merely ghosts, their roars absorbed into the earth.

Reflecting Pool

The pool water glimmered like chips of mined diamonds, just as off limits for the people of the neighborhood. The white couple had snuck in–not being guests of the hotel, but rather working for an NGO–and casually strolled into the pool. Unsuspecting. Their burned white skin blinding under the November sun. One half of the couple dipped toes, the other half of the couple submerged to the armpits. They let the sun dry them off, and strolled out just as casually. Big pillows of gray clouds suffocated the sun, and it smelled like rain.

The couple meandered down the road and walked in single file if a truck roared by. The ABCs of AIDS were painted on the passing billboards. A man pissed on the wall of the information center, a building shaped like a pointy hat, the symbol now chosen to be on the country's flag because the previous image–a warrior–did not reflect the Peaceful Country, the title all schoolchildren now pronounced.

The couple swooped under the bridge as the rain began. An old man with a grizzled chin and hands injected with rope-like veins huddled in a box under the bridge. A clap of thunder–BAM!–and he opened his drifting eyes and said, "Oh shit" the 'i' carried out like an 'e'. Oh sheet.

"Yes, a sheet of rain," one half of the couple said, and the other half didn't laugh. They meandered because now the clouds were cool and soothed their burned skin.

They walked without looking. No longer seeing the children who asked for lipompong or the old women crouched by the popcorn stands. So they didn't notice, meters behind them, a person with a knife. Who had eyes for seeing in the rain.

Peaceful Country

It was supposed to be the Peaceful Country.

But Tom had a gun stuck up in his ribs, shoving the space between the bones. He didn't bleed water. I read about his death in an email, traced his face on CNN. "This is a safe place," the Police Chief said, but only because he had a gun too, slung across his back, the barrel batting his back pocket.

Machina

A pregnant girl is in the shop with ceilings higher than aloe trees. There are shelves she cannot reach because her belly anchors her to the floor and her back bends as she tries to look up and choose a six-month expired box of spaghetti. This is the one store that sells dented boxes of Rice Krispies, and only the white Volunteers with their airmailed marshmallows understand their value. The pregnant girl shuffles in flip-flops and chooses brown bananas and cans of sardines in red sauce, and baked beans and a belly-sized bag of mealie-meal that will feed sixty-seven bellies.

Everyone shops at the Chinese stores. Sometimes guards stand by (black in black). The Machina speak no English but Sesotho. Chinese is their code no one cares to understand. But they all count in English. One-two-three not *ngoe-peli-tharo*. When did numbers stop being fingers and become words?

The Machina are secretive. The girl and her friends used to pull their eyes downwards and pretend they were Machina. The Machina sell twelve different kinds of Cadbury bars. The girl desperately wants a bar with raisins and biscuit bits, but it costs as much as the baby hat that she bought in PEP–the sunken-in, all-purpose store across town.

In a few months she will come back with a baby on her hip, its milky spit up on her dress, fresh bruises along her neck and collarbone, her feet tough as leather for walking the road alone. Her hands grasping the few coins that her father-husband will give her, his cold stare looming in her mind.

The Visits of Lightning

They wrote lies about lightning storms. Penned them in clipped English and curly letters. There was a pick-up game of soccer, one wrote, and he got zapped (though zapped wasn't his word–touched or something) by a jolt of light and it hurt. That's all he wrote: it hurt. Another girl wrote her uncle died from a strike as he herded sheep. On Sunday. But Sunday had been cold and clear, and the night was black and even. They told lies when I asked for truths. When they wrote truths they ate chicken at KFC and bought ice cream and new clothes. When they wrote truths they flew in planes and stood on the edges of shores and looked at water even bluer and deeper than the Katse Dam. When they wrote truths they visited America.

That week a lightning storm ambushed the villages. It tore apart the trees and burned grass. It struck a scared flock of sheep in 'Me Mathabo's yard. And killed them all. She lost six sheep–electrocuted and crispy–and she couldn't eat the flesh because it smelled like sulfur. And that is a truth.

On the Habits of Baboons

Baboons might know that the river is both the physical and political border that separates South Africa from Lesotho. Or Lesotho from South Africa. But in the dark sunsets, they run on their knuckles across the water's surface and eat from the scraps of yards. They are refugees without a permanent home: half the day as immigrants, the other half as emigrants. They cross borders and engage in complex ritual greetings like warriors. They play dead on the sides of roads because they taunt the very cars they try to break into. Their hands like human hands and they flick open car doors and trunks. Baboons steal toasted cheese sandwiches and Flake bars and apples red and bright. And they shit at your feet. They chase birds from their roosts and bellow into the bald night.

But what they are all doing is calling for their mothers.

PART THREE

Evenings With Hilda

I stalk hospital corridors. The doctors don't notice an extra person wandering about, and the hospitals are so understaffed that once I was asked to help give CPR to a woman who had lost her breath. I placed my hands on her chest, thumped her lungs like I was told. It was almost unbearable for me until I felt her life completely extinguished from her body, and my thirst for her lessened. I told the doctor it was all over. He told me to keep trying, and I mimicked the part of the savior. When he was ready, the doctor gave up too.

I stalk the corridors to see the dying. The ones that are moaning to have it end or whose eyelids quiver in pain and hallucination are the best–they'll take any release at this stage. I made it a point, about fifty years ago, to ask them if they want to die. It's the right thing to do–not right for me, because I'm guided by no religious code–but right for them. Because I want them to think they have a choice. And if they say yes, I want to die, I lean over their bedsides and take their lives. I say I don't do this for a religious code (in this Christian pungent country with the dead spirits of relatives residing over the land like a deep fog, I would never say this aloud) because there is no god. Not god in the way people have envisioned it. Their kind of god could never have created me and left me to roam hospitals and kill people. And so, though I know there's no heaven or eternal reward they are getting, at least they will leave with someone having been merciful to them.

Today I come across Ma Ava's room as the priest leaves. I heard the nurses whisper that she has no family, and this is even better, for no one will miss her.

People think someone like me can't control my appetite, but it's an appetite like anyone's. You don't go crazy when you see a fried chicken if you haven't eaten for hours. Perhaps after days or weeks, but I never wait that long.

The hospital wears a dingy overcoat of grey, from dust, disease or dirt–for I rarely see them clean. This hospital is unlike the one in Bloemfontein that I visited once. That one gleamed white and had halls wide enough for two beds. There are sick people in this corridor. They lean over, gasping in wheelchairs, wipe their eyes and groan with snot on cots hastily made, the old sheets tossed aside. I have seen them reuse sheets, if there are no signs of vomit or blood. In the front corridor, by the barely manned front desk, people cluster. Babies are slung across their mothers, and there is no end to the tears, coughs and mucus.

I edge closer to the door. A doctor swishes past me, his coat is open and slightly grimy, and it fans out as though he is walking into some mysterious wind, and the shrieks and coughs in the background make me think that he is indeed a hero, a soldier emerging from the battlefield, and if you look closely, you might see his battle wounds: the bloodshot eyes of sleeplessness, the bite marks, the tense nerves. He goes past me, and as is so common for me now, barely registers me. When he passes, I duck into Ma Ava's room.

I like to look at the medical charts to see what they're dying from. Though these are written in code. Not of another alphabet or number system, but a system where one disease means another. Not because they want to be deceitful or because they are unsure, but because how does one write AIDS and have that on the official death certificate, especially when it was the TB or the flu or a headache that pushed them over? Her chart says TB. This is the most common, but she has been here for six weeks, and they're afraid they'll lose her any day.

She is a woman who was once large, big-boned and insulated with thick plump fat (which can be more difficult for me, harder to get down to the veins). But the layers of fat sag in folds around her, the face is skeletal. She is resting, her breath light puffs, and her closed eyelids purple. I lean next to her and take her hand. She doesn't move. "Ma Ava," I whisper, not wanting to startle her because I only want them to be calm. Their fear can increase my hunger, but if she's calm, I'll be calm. "Ma Ava, what would make you happy right now?"

Her lips lightly smack as though she has finished a good meal. I take that as answer enough. "Lefu, you say?

I'll oblige." I sweep back her hair, cradle her chin, and turn her head away from me, exposing the plane of thin-fleshed neck, the jugular pulsing like a distant ticking bomb. And then I bite her neck.

Hilda sits in front of the radio when I return home. She doesn't live with me because people would talk, and the constant temptation might be too much for me. She lives next door with her cousin and the cousin's boyfriend but spends time in my kitchen, cooking food so that the smells float out and people think I eat, and she listens to my radio and likes to sing along into the cooking spoon. We talk about the day, and this is how I keep my sanity.

"Rasta music, listen to those beats." She plays the bowls, turned upside down on their lips. "If you listen close enough you can feel the beach."

I settle down on the sofa, my belly full, and my skin more lustrous than it had been that morning. It was like a meal and exercise all in one. "How was your day?" This is how our conversations always begin.

"Hamonate. I saw a flurry of cyclists down King's Road. I met a really nice lady from Cape Town. She's working at the Embassy. We went for a coffee."

"Very cultured day."

"Mmm." She turns up the radio and gets up to make tea. The water boils in time to her rocking hips, the jiving music. "How was your day?" she asks when the tea is made, and she and I sit with our mugs. She laps at the heat with her tongue, and I hold the mug close to my throat, resting it on my collarbone because I discovered long ago that burning liquids against my skin almost feels like the heat I get from being near a dying person. I'm still riding high on Ma Ava.

"One TB patient today."

"Man or woman?" This is a detail Hilda always likes to know. I think she mentally keeps track of this statistic and would get on my case if I wasn't being equal to the sexes. Hilda is progressive in her own way, and this is part of the reason why she is not married.

"Woman. Middle-aged."

"Did she cry?" Hilda also takes an interest in people's reactions, but I don't like to answer this. Hilda is the only person who knows about me, but there are some things that I still don't like to talk about with her.

"There was almost a cancer patient, but he passed before I could get close."

"Lots of family?"

"*Ee*, many." Actually, only a bitter grown-child but Hilda wants to believe that people are loved.

I have lived in this same place as long as Hilda's been alive–thirty-two years now. Her grandma used to live next door to me, and when she died, Hilda moved in with her cousin. She was twelve then. But she had visited her grandma every Sunday until her death. They would go to church together and come back for dinner, and I would sit on the other side of the fence that separated our houses and listen to Hilda tell her grandma stories.

Once the grandma told Hilda that she was sick, and soon the good Lord would give her some relief, and that she wasn't afraid but looking forward to it. That evening, I crept into the grandma's house and in her sleep–through her dreams–I asked if she wanted to die. She murmured yes, and I bit her neck, but as I dabbed the blood from the corners of my mouth, I looked up and Hilda was staring at me from the doorway. She had decided to stay the night in case the good Lord took her grandma then, and I hadn't noticed her slumbering in the sitting room.

I had only bitten a healthy child once–in my early days. Hilda did not scream or faint at the sight of her grandmother dying, and surprisingly, she didn't look at me in horror. All she said was, "So you do the good Lord's work?"

And that's how she found out.

I made a conscious effort to never harm her. I sit away from her in the house and have her scrub the dishes with bleach, so no scent of her stays behind like an afterthought. I never accept tea from her hands, so she places it on the table. When she was growing up, I'd talk to her through the fence, and she used to drape a scarf around her neck.

When she first came to my door, not too long after her grandmother's funeral, I staggered backwards and lifted my dirty work shirt up to my nose. It was her lack of fear that finally allowed me to let her in.

Nobody else knows about me, but people are intuitive, so I am not well liked and rarely approached. Not by shopkeepers or beggars, children or elders, not by animals–especially not by the skittish horses. Sometimes people cross the street if I come by, and I stopped riding public transport for two reasons: the scent of blood gave me headaches, and no one seemed to ever sit by me. During the day I am rarely spoken to, and so evenings with Hilda are wonderful.

I masquerade as a landfill worker. This helps to fill my days and give me money, not that I have much need for it for myself, but I sometimes like to surprise Hilda. I learned not to give her things too often, for that wide, teary smile I so cherish will fade with too many offerings. So I make them few and build up the weeks and months until I can see the smile and know that I am the pendulum that knocks that smile into place.

There is a specific reason I chose the landfill job–the only reason in fact–all the smells block out the smell of blood. And people stay away from you when you reek of moldy mealie meal, bread crusts, throw-up, tea bags, rotten tomatoes, soiled clothes, baby shit, cut hairs, dirty tissues, hot sauce, rubber, candle ends, empty sardine cans.

I do my job half-heartedly because there is so much garbage, and my job never seems to end, and I never seem to a make a dent in it. Children come here too. Sometimes with their thin mothers, picking through the waste for scraps of clothing. I go through and pick up dead batteries and paint cans, and the needles and razors secretly tossed here by the clothing company nearby. Sometimes I am told to burn trash, and the chemicals that are hidden in it burn so intensely that the sky turns black, and the children's eyes weep.

Oftentimes I leave early and head to the clinics, the hospitals, even the streets. Homeless are dying all of the time, and these are the ones that nobody misses; though because they are out in public they are harder to kill. Once I almost got caught. I had stumbled upon a young man in an alley, behind the public restroom of a petrol station. He was hacking up blood, and I wanted to get down on my knees and lick it up, feel that sticky metal sweetness on my tongue, between my teeth, against my gums.

I had asked him what was wrong, and he couldn't say anything, just grabbed his throat. And his face was wet, his legs bent beneath him, and he looked broken for someone so young, and I asked him if he wanted to die, and he nodded. I bit him, and blood spurted from his mouth, and I put my hands over it so that I could get as much as possible.

"Hey," someone had shouted. Another young boy

stood with a knife in his hand, and he looked terrified. That's the face I never want to see. "Mmolai. Murderer," he yelled, and I knew that there were people beyond the alley, in close reach, so I took a rock and threw it at his head. Then I bit him too.

Hilda usually smells of fresh laundry. She washes towels and linens at a foreign embassy and brings the smell of hot soap with her. I like to watch her hands flicker from stove to kettle to table, dry ridges imbedded in her palms and knuckles, the skin puckered in little kisses. She isn't ashamed of the work.

She leads her stories with her maestro pointer-finger and speckles the air with her fingertips. "I overheard a funny conversation today at work…." She gets the words out, and her hands are birds in front of her face.

"You don't say." I close my eyes to hear better everything she says.

I only see Hilda in the context of my home. I have never seen her walk down the street or buy oranges from the old lady who sits under the bridge. Have never watched her smooth back her hair in front of the shop windows, pretending to fix herself up, while she admires new shoes and stereos. Sometimes when I walk the streets, I imagine she walks next to me, quickly because her legs are short, her hands hovering near her face as she discusses the inner lives of the people on the street, or the book she is reading (she gets them free from her cousin, a school teacher who steals discarded paperbacks flown in from charities).

If I walked with Hilda, I would take her past my route, past the cold hospital doors, around the restaurant in the building shaped like a hat. I would point out to her the young people who have taken to wearing black shirts that scream in red letters: I AM POSITIVE, their smiles a bit strained as they pass. We would crouch under the windows of the bakery and inhale the smell of bread, then weave in and out of the roving vehicles in a winding dance back home.

Later that week, I come home, and Hilda is not there. There have been times when she hasn't been waiting for me but either has told me about her prior plans, or it was an emergency, like when her cousin had a miscarriage. I make tea and sit in the silence we associate with the lack of sound when the radio is not on. She doesn't come and the night falls, and because I never have to sleep, I go outdoors and watch Hilda's home through the spaces in the fence. I watch until morning, and my bones hurt, so I skip work and head to hospital for nourishment.

That evening I come back later than usual, but Hilda is there. She is folding paper flowers out of glossy magazine pages. A small bouquet rests among the clutter of tea things. She does every fold deliberately and crisply and doesn't take her eyes off of her work to look at me.

"Ho joang?" She speaks nonchalantly.

"Where were you yesterday?"

"I've already made tea." She nods her head towards the table.

"I don't care about tea, but I want to know."

"Believe me, you'll need a cup of tea. It's best if you hear this when you're calm."

I take the tea, frustrated, and sit opposite her at the table. I dabble my fingers on the surface of the tea.

"Mona, take a flower." She presses one into my hand. "They are for my cousin's birthday. I'm going to decorate the house to surprise her." She looks off into nether-space. "She has always wanted a garden."

"Hilda."

"Yesterday I found out that I'm positive."

"Positive?"

"Honestly." She puts a flower into my teacup, right between my fingers, and the paper soaks up the moisture and shrinks. "I have HIV. And it's far along."

"How...is that possible?"

"Are you really asking me that? Think about it."

I know there must be boyfriends. Hilda's fairly pretty–except for wide-set eyes that not everyone likes and one arm slightly shorter than the other–but she is a woman, and that's all that some men care about.

"What are you going to do, Hilda?"

Now she looks at me. She pushes the flowers off to the side. "We both know the answer to that."

"You can't mean that."

"I do."

I dunk the flower all the way into the tea. She reaches her hands out towards me but doesn't touch me; that would be too much. And I have always wanted to feel Hilda, but I love her too much to do that to either of us. I once rested my hands on the back of her neck–deep between the shoulder blades–and I had to run from the house and to keep running until it was dark, and when I had gone back, Hilda had left. We never talk about that night.

"Listen to me. This is what you have promised to do. Don't you want to help people?"

"I can't do this to you, Hilda."

She stands up. "To me? *For* me."

"Forgive me for being selfish, but I don't want to come home and not have you here."

"What about what I want? I'm going to get old. I'm always going to be sick. Sheba." She points to the fleshy part of her underarm, and there is a deep open sore. "It's starting. I'm going to die, and you never will."

This wasn't completely true. I could die. But as long as I keep feeding, I won't die. This is an important detail.

"It doesn't have to be now."

"Don't you get it?" Her arms flail. "You don't," she says softly. "You can't because death is not a reality for you."

"Not a reality for me? I see death all the time. I touch the dying."

"So touch me."

I smash the teacup against the wall. She doesn't even flinch. "I don't want to."

Hilda gets up close to my face. I can smell her, see the wisps of hair that frizz around her ears, two differently shaped pointy ears. She breathes on me. "You have always wanted to. And if you don't, you will see me wilt. I will crumble, rotting with disease. I won't be able to sit here with you. I can't afford the medicine."

"I'll buy you..."

"No. I don't want any suffering. I just want to die peacefully. When I'm still young. Pretty. Happy. When men still want me."

I'm not sure I can promise her peace. I don't know if all of those I help feel pain with the bites. I like to think they don't.

"It's late," she says. She leaves me standing there, clenching my fists, biting my lips. The smell of Hilda lingers on.

The house without Hilda feels like a finished cup of tea, the heat still lingering at the bottom, the handle cold and smooth. It is like finding abandoned hospital beds, the sheets wrinkled, because someone hasn't come yet to take them away. I don't want to stay, so I leave and go to hospital. But this is the time of night when it's too quiet, so I must walk purposefully as though I am visiting someone I know. I duck into the room farthest from the nurse's station, and there is a young woman hooked up to an IV, her veins pushing through her skin. She is awake.

"Hello," I say, because the space needs something.

She doesn't look away from the ceiling, her eyes fixed in their sockets, water welling up in the delicate skin of her inner eyelids. She breathes through her mouth, and her bottom teeth are missing.

There isn't a chair in the room, so I crouch by her bedside. I stroke her fingers, and they twitch.

"What are you looking at?"

I get nothing from her. I move the wristband that she wears until I can see her name: Palesa. It means flower. Why must dying take away beauty? Wear it out until it is only alive through machines? The IV drips, slowly and planned.

"Would you like your eyes to be closed forever?" Her tongue plays with the holes in her mouth, but she doesn't respond.

"Excuse me." I felt the presence the moment he entered the room. I turn around, and the priest is there, his Bible in one hand, the other clasping rosary beads.

"She's dying," I tell him.

He nods. "That's why I'm here."

I notice that he trembles as he stands. I get up, move past him, and flee quickly from the building.

I have watched the priest from Nigeria—a tall drip of black ink—leaking from patient to patient. He visits those who don't have much longer, who dwell in the ditch between this present heart-beating world and the passive bleakness of death. He tells them beaded prayers in whispers that a supposed God–and I–could hear. And when he leaves, I go in. But now he is not paying any visits. Not since the other day. He stays at home near the church. I have no fear of crosses. To be stretched out and resting on a wooden beam–that is how I'd want to die– watching the world I never knew below my feet. I always like to think of the priest as my brother, ushering out the dead.

The church is dark and cool and plain, the walls bare, the church pews rigid. He sits alone in the middle of the church. I take a seat next to him and fold my hands.

"I've been waiting for you," he says.

Maybe he has seen me lurking. Or maybe this is what he says to all people whom he thinks have come to confess.

"I'm not here to pray," I tell him.

He nods. His eyes are yellow and weeping; his voice cracks when he speaks. "Even I have grown weary from asking God." He bows his head, and the cross around his neck swings. I place my hands on his throat. He sways towards me, his head near my chest where I have so often wanted Hilda to rest her own. He smells of salt.

I shove his slumped body onto his knees, resting his head on the pew in front of us. I take the cross from around his neck. I have never taken anything from anyone before.

My evenings are empty pockets of time. I boil water until the kettle shrieks. I lie on the sofa and stare at the ceiling, count the tiles, and replay all of my old conversations with Hilda. I wear the cross around my neck now, and this makes me feel like a human. Believing in the unseen, I rub my hand across the silver face, and I can almost believe in magic.

Two weeks go by, and Hilda doesn't come to visit. I make tea, but it's lonely. I listen to the radio, but the voices annoy me. Today I killed an old alcoholic, who asked for God's release, and the taste of him seems foul now.

So I send Hilda a letter: *I'm sorry. Please visit.*

She comes by the next day. I haven't eaten, and I am sitting by the window when she opens the door. "How was your day?" she says.

I don't pretend to be surprised. "Uneventful. No one since yesterday."

"Mang?"

"An alcoholic."

"How kind of you."

"And yours?"

"I've been reading a play. *Hamlet.* Tragic, everyone dies."

"My kind of story."

She manages a smile for me. "Would you like me to tell you about it?"

"Please."

When I put her to bed that night, I will ask her what I have asked them all. She'll answer because that's what she has planned.

"Let me make you a cup of tea," she says and then begins to tell me about the play.

I memorize Hilda's movements. She fills the kettle from the bucket by the door, wipes it off on her skirt before placing it on the burner, turns on the gas, and it click-clicks. She fiddles with the radio and sets out two matching mugs, talking about Shakespeare in between snatches of songs she hums. I watch her hands conduct the makings of tea. She places a tea bag in each mug, arranges crumbly, butter-yellow biscuits onto the only plate I own.

I make a wish that time will move slowly tonight, so I can feel every moment. I will keep her talking as she climbs into bed and will remember the shape of her lips as she speaks. I will gather those paper flowers she made and place them by her side. I will read from *Hamlet* in place of any prayer and rest the cross in her dried out hands.

I will hope that there's a god for her.

An Apocalyptic Search for Water

I do not hear anyone. I hear things, lots of things. The sound of red grasshoppers and the wind weeping. I hear the birds peck at the sheet-metal roof. But I hear no one because as far as I know—and I know only what I know—I am the one. Only one. Alone one. It wasn't always like this. In the past—longer than a week past but less than a month—there were people in the village. And more people in the lowlands.

I had been sick and had gone to the clinic. An hour walk away. And when I arrived it was full of emptiness. The dark, lonely light bulb swung from the top of the room. I didn't know what to do. I lay on the doctor's table, cold like rain, and shivered. I slept in wild dreamland, and when I woke up there was no one.

Here is what I dreamed, for if they were realities they floated away before I could touch them. Dreams of pigs perched in the thatch and green clouds that rained money and drowned the children. Floozy-flimsy fabrics of pinks and golds and devil's lips red that piled in the rivers and I swam among them but felt nothing. And a man in silver clothes with black ragged teeth tried to bite my fingers, but I ran and grew airplane wings and was about to crash into the highest mountain—Dragon Mountain—and it breathed flames. And that woke me up.

There is no one. Not the doctor or the nurse. Not the schoolchildren or the sangoma with his ancestral hands. Not the coughing donkeys or the scared sheep. I am alone. Alone and lonely are two English words I never could understand when I was in school. But I get them now. Lonely is *feeling*. I feel lonely when I see married couples and when I sit with the young girls. I feel lonely when I do the washing by myself and hear the laughter of men coming from the bareng.

But alone. That is *being*. And when I look outside of the clinic door, I see the rocky hills and dying aloe trees. But I hear no one. And this is what it means to be alone.

I wake up thirsty. My throat burns like scorched sunlight. I want-want-want water. There is a drought. I remember that from the world before. When there were still people in it. I think I slept for days because the shadow-shapes on the floor are different, and the aloes are taller than before.

There is nothing for me to take from the clinic. The drawers are scattered with bandages and cotton balls and one bottle of clear liquid that smells like kerosene. There is a bottle with nothing inside, but a deep crack runs along the bottom. There is a rusted knife, but when I pick it up the blade falls off. It tings on the floor, and I jump. Adding noise to the world seems unfamiliar.

So I hum as I walk so noises cannot bounce at me.

The well outside of the clinic is dry, and I pull the bucket up, and there is a snake. It hisses into a coil of scales, and I dump it back down the well. Only snakes survive in times like these. Walking to my home village is the only thing I can think—in my dried out brain—think to do.

I find the first dead body in a taxi. It crashed into a boulder, and the front door is pushed in like colored-clay.

It is a taxi full of people. And one pig whose neck is twisted. They smell of rancid meat and vomit. Like a sick-ick-ickiness. And I throw up. My raw, dry throat burns. And I am too dry to even cry tears. The driver's eyes are wide open, like his eyelids were pulled apart and pinned to his skin. The taxi crackles with noise. I lift my skirt up to my face and cover my nose. Hunching down on my knees, I reach in, past the driver's face, and I touch the radio. I hear voices. And they speak English and my own language. And crackle: *Lefu…death…no one knows how many people*. I keep listening. The voice keeps playing over and over and over: *The date is Sunday*. I arrived at the clinic on a Sunday. It is recorded. The voices are not speaking now. They are in the past like all of the people.

I don't know who I am now. And I'm not sure that will even matter again. I say my name aloud just to hear it being said. I say my name over and over—overover— until it doesn't sound like my name anymore and becomes new. I say the name of my village—and I'm close to it now—but that name doesn't matter because there's not even a sign to let people know which huts are my village and which are another. And so that name gets lost too. I puff the name out to the air, which may be alive with disease, and it dies. I kill all the names I know.

This is how I spend my time until I get to my village–nameless and people-less–and my hut door is wide open, and my mother is dead inside. She is bent on the floor like all of her bones are broken. I clearly see her left hand, palm up and fingers curled. This is how she would reach for me when I was younger, taking my hand to drag me through the roads.

I can't go in.

I wail at the doorstep until I have no more sound. I already forget what she looks like because I can only see her body crumpled, her one hand outstretched.

There are matches and kerosene in the second hut where we cook. And the thatch is dry because this is drought season. I shut the door and burn the house. And this is how I bury my mother.

And maybe this is my mission, to burn all of the dead like God's hell angel. But the smoke chokes me, and I remember water is my mission. So I leave my dead village.

Water comes from the mountains. Even the children know this, and that is why we look to the skies in drought. Not for rain but we look up to the mountain peaks because all water is stored there. Even the clouds take the water from the mountains and give it back to us as rain. And so it is the mountains we look to.

I have never been to Dragon Mountain. But that is

the tallest and where I must go.

Moisture-sucked roads lead upwards, and my climb is slow. Slower than sunbeams crossing the sky. In the first day my body becomes awake. I see a lizard clutching the side of a rock, and I pick up a brother-rock and try to smash it, but it escapes. There is a trickle of water coming from a spout at a village pump. I trust my ears more, and I hear it before I see it. I stumble on the ground, my knees resting against the pump, my skirt pushed between my legs as I bend my head and slurp-slurp the spider-web thin strain of water.

Temptation. Like first kisses and stolen bites of chocolate—I want more—can feel the water on my tongue and now my throat rages. Fire-fire-put it out. And I must continue.

I fall asleep in the rough patch of grass that sleeps by the pump.

Grrr. I wake up, and there, bent low to the ground, is a gut-grey dog showing his teeth. In this world there are no longer masters, and the dogs run wild. But there are still rocks. God can kill us all; the sun can burn us up, but rocks will stay. The devil's playthings, my mother called them, because they could kill the crops and a man's head.

I gather some gravel near my head and yell, "Skit-skat anta!" and throw the crushed roughness at its face. It runs. Because lintja are cowards.

I walk all day. Walking like I have nothing else to do. I can't feel my tongue. I lick my teeth and feel nothing.

The mountains are getting bigger, the road is longer, and now I walk up–because water is kept up high like birds' eggs–drop drop drops of life–but if water falls it does not crack but spreads, and it can be licked up. It isn't gone once it's found.

Here it's harder to breathe, chest sweating and I wipe my hands across my breastbone and lick the sweat from it. It does not cool, and now my mouth is salty. Only looking at the ground as I walk and I see the rocks of dried dung-color. There–see there–a group of sheep dead on their sides, a stiff lamb trying to reach its mother's nipple.

I sleep that night in a donga, and it keeps out the wind.

In the morning my back roars, and I crawl on hands and knees until I feel like standing. Come back to me memories, remind me of when I drank from buckets and lay in cool huts and smelled cooking food. Remind me of taste and conversations. Remind me of the world before it died. And somehow I forget I am walking, and I touch Dragon Mountain. There are no signs, but it is tall, and it is big, and I am here. So it is. Crawling again. Will the sun set? Will I see it set?

The higher I get, the harder it is to breathe. The air is thinner around my throat, thicker around the sun. The rocks hurt beneath my fingers, burrow into my knees. The snakes do not slither here. In my head, I see them slithering about the ashes of my mother. I stop, forehead to the ground.

And then listen carefully.

I hear water. I follow my ears, and beyond that rock that looks like all others, there is a waterfall. And it falls into a stream that follows the opposite mountainside. And I cup my hands like little bowls and scoop the water into my mouth and feel for the first time, a long time, and drink and I drink, drink.

The sound of water in my ears.

The Ashen Shoes

One time, not too distant from right now, there was a young woman with a troubled face. Her eyes squinted up and over the ridge of her nose because she studied the cooking ashes too deeply. That was how it appeared to her fat mother and her thin sister. But what she was really doing was saying English words in her head, studying the way the letters looked in her clear and present mind. Because, though she wasn't given any opportunities to write, she wrote in her mind.

She liked to write her name—'Maseeiso–into the English words that sounded like Ma, say so! She imagined a small child–a boy in her mind because she always wanted a son–eager and bouncy (not like the small, sad boys who herded animals in Lesotho's mountains) calling to her: *Ma, say so!* And she'd respond, *I say so!* and laugh, even though no good child would ever call his mother anything but *'me*.

'Maseeiso dreamt of English words in the morning, after the breakfast fires died down and her older sister, Eugenia, had gone off to the secondary school where she got to flaunt English words all day long to the children she taught. Eugenia had perfected her English. She used to sit behind British ministers and tourists and mimic their words. She spellbound the students with her accent.

'Maseeiso, the youngest, never got to finish school. For who would take care of Eugenia's baby? And what about 'Maseeiso's father and his second wife whom she called mother only out of formality? Someone spry and strong had to get water and cook and beat out the mice from the roof and sweep the yard and…all the other things. People had younger children to do these things or so 'Maseeiso's mother said.

Eugenia had a real job. She had a luxury in all this boring poverty. And she had taken her English name—Eugenia—and discarded the other. "All people will be able to pronounce my name," she had explained to 'Maseeiso. "I can relate to everyone."

It occurred to neither Eugenia nor 'Maseeiso that "everyone" only included their own.

'Maseeiso's grandmother had once told them about Eugenia's naming day—a special day floating among ordinary ones—when the baby (after one brave year in this physical world) was blessed with a name. And for girls, a name they would have until they were married (and their mothers-in-law would rename them). Names were given with purpose, grandmother had told them. But it was natural for them to change because with the ancestors' goodwill, they would change and grow up. On Eugenia's naming day she had sobbed until the priest suggested a Christian name. And when Eugenia was given that name, she stopped crying. A true sign, grandmother had told them, that Eugenia was a modern woman of the world.

It wasn't in 'Maseeiso's nature to complain. She didn't cry much as a child, didn't protest when her parents pulled her out of school, and didn't resent them when they made her take care of the house. Though she was not without her strengths. When little boys would throw rocks at the harmless kittens that wandered alone, she would rescue them and singe the boys with her threats. When her father hit her second mother, she stepped in and took the beatings instead. Though her mother would retreat to the chicken coop and pretend to feed the chickens, ignoring 'Maseeiso. 'Maseeiso was many things, but she was not weak.

One afternoon–in the late summer when winds were picking up and the sun didn't reach as high in the sky– Eugenia came home from school in a flurry. 'Maseeiso sat with a troubled face, stirring porridge over the fire. She was in the midst of mentally reciting a poem she had read from a sneak peek in one of Eugenia's schoolbooks, when Eugenia interrupted.

"I have wonderful news, Mother." She plopped her books down on the front stoop and absently patted the head of her baby who was strapped to 'Maseeiso's back. "I have heard that there is going to be a party to celebrate the engagement of the King. And they are inviting families with unmarried children in the hopes of matchmaking."

"Dear God," their mother said, not straying from her chair. "This is indeed wonderful."

Eugenia was almost certain that her status as a teacher would secure an invitation. They told 'Maseeiso to make something special for dinner that night, so she boiled some potatoes and made a meat stew out of the tough lamb that died a few days earlier.

The following week Eugenia received an invitation. It came as a taxi note and was addressed only to her and her parents. Eugenia shrugged apologetically when she read it. "Too bad, 'Maseeiso. But I've heard they asked only school graduates. The King cares very much about education. And they were able to get these names from the exam rosters."

'Maseeiso smiled, looking down at the ground. "No problem, Eugenia."

Her mother shoved her out of the way to get a better look at the note. "It is more important for Eugenia to find a husband. She has a baby to care for. And a husband will be pleased with a wife who has a good job."

"Then what do I have?"

"Excuse me?" Her mother almost spit–her wet tongue quivering in her mouth like she might spit fire.

"What do I have to offer a husband?"

"Some things are not about you." Mother took the invitation and proceeded into the next room to discuss details with Eugenia.

'Maseeiso began to clean up. She worked rhythmically, moving to the meter of the poem in her head.

The celebration was in a week, and so for the next few days Eugenia discussed fabrics and textures and because there was little money, she took apart both her good dress and 'Maseeiso's and hired a woman in the village to make her a new one. She spent a little money on a new pair of shoes–shiny red ones with little bows. Her feet didn't quite fit into them, but Eugenia managed to squeeze. The dress was a collage of red and blue with a white flowered pattern drifted throughout. Her sleeves were puffed, and the skirt ballooned away from her waist, making it look tiny. She sewed a wire in the bodice so that her breasts were uplifted and young again (for the baby had sucked them limp).

'Maseeiso oversaw the preparations with frustration. She began to recite a new poem, one she had made up, and caught herself midway in a smile when she invented the lines: "and the sister was a peacock/overdressed and plucked/with laughter like a squawk."

"Stop smiling," her mother reprimanded. "There is nothing funny here. And the baby is crying."

On the day of the celebration, many young people from the village–some with their parents in tow–clambered into the taxis or in the beds of local pickups, and a few late arrivals walked, carrying their shoes. As a teacher, Eugenia got the front seat of a taxi. Her hair woven in thin braids, decorated with beads, her cheeks rouged, her dress cascading in bright colored hues like wet paints. Men cooed at her, but she turned away, gleaming.

'Maseeiso's parents went along. Amidst car horns and screams of delight, 'Maseeiso sunk to the dirt floor of the doorway and watched them disappear, a trail of dust the only goodbye she got. They had even taken the baby because Eugenia wanted to show off her good mother-rearing skills. And her ability to make beautiful babies.

'Maseeiso feared she would cry–something she never let herself do. So she crept to the fire which had quickly died out. The ashes were still warm, and she began to stir them to life. Her head couldn't even think of words, and in this loss she began to cry into the ashes.

"There's no need to cry."

"Hey!" She turned around, embarrassed at being spied on.

An old woman stood in the doorway, her face in shadow because the sun was bright behind her. She got caught on her words and spoke like a rash–rough and itchy–out of the corner of her mouth. She leaned on a twisted wooden cane, and 'Maseeiso smelled the hint of rosemary. Then she wondered if this was the witch doctor. 'Maseeiso had never met her, but tales of her magic seeped into all homes in the district. Some said she concocted the best love potions that came tied up in ribbons and smelling of metals. It was once said she had brought a dead chief back to life and had cured an entire family of tuberculosis when medical doctors couldn't. Though this hadn't worked for 'Maseeiso's own mother and, therefore, she doubted her powers. 'Maseeiso remembered hearing that the witch doctor had one blind eye that saw beyond normal sight.

"Go away."

The woman stumbled into the hut. "Is that any way to talk to someone who wants to help you?"

'Maseeiso looked closely at her face now. Her right eye looked pickled, and 'Maseeiso knew for certain that this was the witch doctor. "I don't need any help."

"You want to go to the celebration, no?"

"I wasn't invited."

"I'm not asking if you were invited. I'm asking you if you want to go."

'Maseeiso hugged her knees and turned away so the woman wouldn't see her tears. "It doesn't matter what I want because I can't go."

The witch hobbled further into the room and crouched near 'Maseeiso. The scent of rosemary was overpowering. "Ah, but that is your problem, 'Maseeiso. It does matter. Everyone's wants matter. And you can't go?" she sputtered. "Only you are stopping yourself."

It didn't strike 'Maseeiso as anything out of the ordinary that the witch knew her name. She *was* a witch. And this was a small village. The witch had found her, after all, and it occurred to 'Maseeiso that the witch had been looking specifically for her.

"It's too late to go now."

"Ah." The witch swung her cane into the air. "It is

never too late."

"I don't have a dress."

The witch waved the cane. "Details. Small details."

"And how will I get there?"

"Shush. It can be done. If—" The witch leaned closer, sucking in her cheeks so her lips pouted out. "If you believe it can be done."

'Maseeiso thought of her poems and the dozens of words tangled in her mind and Eugenia. "I believe."

The witch squealed. "Very good." She helped 'Maseeiso stand up. "Bring me the best dress you have."

'Maseeiso slumped. "Eugenia cut it up."

"Bring me what is left."

'Maseeiso gathered the shreds of her dress and laid them at the witch's feet. The witch gathered dust and added water in a bowl then rubbed the clay-like mixture along the seams. In the dusky rays of the lowering sun, 'Maseeiso saw a faint glow—like pollen on moth wings—piercing through the mud. The witch bent down and shook out the dress and after a few flaps, the dress was whole.

"Oh my," breathed 'Maseeiso, reaching to touch the fabric. The dress had a new life and was an intense violet color unlike any dress 'Maseeiso had seen before. The witch fitted the dress over 'Maseeiso's head. It swept over her breasts, revealing her defined collarbone, and tucked around her waist, then flowed out from her hips, stopping at her calves.

The witch led her outdoors. An old horse was tied up in the neighboring yard. "Here is your ride, 'Maseeiso."

"That horse is so old, it can barely carry a bag of grain."

"Is it?" She went over and loosened the rope, and then clicked her tongue, beckoning the horse to follow. As it approached 'Maseeiso, she saw it transform. With each blink of her eyes the horse seemed to shed layers of age, the strong muscles rippled, the head less bent. Now, with this blink, the back leg didn't drag, and the coat was whiter. Here, with this blink of the eyes, he expanded with a heavy layer of fat. The eyes were less red and watery; instead, they were bright, and it appeared to 'Maseeiso that he was a hand or two taller than she remembered. The horse that nudged her shoulder was strong and beautiful and moonlight-colored, and she thought maybe it was the moon that was doing this and rubbed her eyes.

"Your eyesight is fine, 'Maseeiso." The witch patted the horse's haunches. "Now you have a ride, and a dress and here——" She pulled from her wool cape a woven basket. "This is a gift you can give to the King. To show your gratitude."

'Maseeiso clutched it tenderly and wrapped it up in her hair scarf. Her closely shaved head cooled down in the early evening air. She rarely had her head uncovered, and it felt liberating.

The witch placed her palms on 'Maseeiso's soft

cheeks and blew on her. "For luck." She smiled, and 'Maseeiso saw that her two front teeth were silver.

"Please," 'Maseeiso touched the old hands. "This is all very wonderful, I am so thankful—"

"But?"

'Maseeiso pointed at her feet. They stuck out beneath the violet dress, dirty in flattened men's boots. "I can't wear these. Everyone will be able to tell I don't belong."

The witch just laughed. "Child, of course I can fix that. Just a little oversight." She took 'Maseeiso's hand and led her back into the cooking hut. There was a bucket of water for washing, and she dipped a bowl into it and poured it into the cooling ashes. Her hands —crooked but quick—shaped the wet ash into two lumps. The inside of the hut was dark now, and 'Maseeiso didn't bother to light the paraffin lamp, and the generator was out of fuel.

As her eyes adjusted to the dark, she saw that the witch was sculpting shoes. There was a heel. Now, the point and a deep crest for what appeared to be a bow. Perfectly identical. The witch picked them up and blew on them; the ashes snowed on the ground revealing two stunning silver shoes with glistening bows of silk and tall heels. They were narrow with long points, delicate and star-like.

"They're beautiful."

The witch helped her take off the boots. 'Maseeiso scrubbed her feet with water and soap, afraid of putting any dirt inside of the shoes. When they were placed on her feet, she stood up tall and felt in that moment–for the first time ever–that she was a beautiful woman.

"Lovely," said the witch, satisfied with her work. She helped 'Maseeiso onto the horse, and before she rode off to the party (the horse knowing the way, the witch said with a wink), the witch passed on some advice. "You must remember, 'Maseeiso, that you can have the dress, the horse and the shoes, but how tonight goes is up to you. Even the gods need a helping hand once in awhile." She stroked the shoes. "These will only keep for tonight. When the sun passes over the night sky, they will return to ash. Everything has an end."

She gave the horse a swat on the hind, and 'Maseeiso was off to the party.

The party throbbed with joyful music in the basin of a valley. Paper lanterns were hooked onto trees and fences; a huge white tent sprawled in the center where the hub of dancing was located. Tables of food, served by pleasant plump women, smelled of meat fat and sauces and fresh bread, and the heavy smell of *joala* made everyone drunk without even tasting it. A band played with fiddles, accordions, and hand drums. A harmonica shrieked over it all, and there was laughter, hollering, and the chattering of good conversations, with the undertones of fun flirtations. Women were dressed in vibrant primary colors and deep chocolate browns, and the men had immaculate white shirts and bleached shoes, their pants starched, a few wrapped in rich red and black blankets. Everyone was crisp and clean and smiling.

'Maseeiso arrived in the midst of fireworks. The sky almost paled in comparison to the throng of color below. When 'Maseeiso rode in on her horse, the crowd parted, and some even thought a princess had arrived. Perhaps a long-lost relative of the royal family. *Did the King take a second wife?* some asked. *Not very Christian but who would question the royal family?* Men reached out to touch the firmness of the horse, women to touch the hem of her dress.

English words swirled in her head when she tried to describe the scene before her. A treasure trove of adjectives percolated on her tongue: succulent, pulsating, glimmering, colorful, jubilant. At the white tent, she got off the horse—helped down by two eager, friendly older men. She entered the tent, and the music spun magic around all of the dancers. She joined a circle of women and in moments found herself in the center, spinning like a crazy flower being twirled by the fingertips of children. She had never laughed so much in her life. She moved her shoulders, swung her hips, and spotted Eugenia beaming among several young men.

One man, tall and smooth-skinned, slid away from her sister and plucked 'Maseeiso from the group of women and danced with her. "What's your name?" he asked her. When he smiled—and he did this often as he talked—his eyes brightened, fit snugly above his round cheeks.

"'Maseeiso." His name was Edmund, and he spoke rich English and would interchange words freely. 'Maseeiso realized that she, too, had been speaking in English.

"What do you do, 'Maseeiso?"

"Do?" She hesitated. She still knew she was the same woman underneath–that the witch's magic couldn't change the history of her person.

He squeezed her hand as he spun her about. "Yes. Do. In your village."

"I...I cook and take care of my niece and my parents."

"You are very busy."

"It's not anything."

He grinned. "Doesn't sound like it. It sounds like you are the foundation of your family. But—" And here 'Maseeiso feared he would unravel her secret. "But what do you do when you're not taking care of anyone?"

She had never been asked this before, and in being asked, 'Maseeiso's thoughts suddenly bloomed outward. "I write poetry. I love to play with words."

Edmund laughed, and 'Maseeiso felt both warm and nervous. "That's wonderful. I teach literature at the University."

"You do?" 'Maseeiso had never met anyone as well educated as he, and though Eugenia was smart, she didn't have a chance at University.

"Who do you read?" he asked.

"Anything I can find."

They had stopped dancing and now sat on hay bales. Edmund spread his jacket on one for her to sit upon.

"Your favorite poem?"

No one had ever asked her this. "There are so many."

He smiled. "Then tell me about them all."

They spoke of poetry, and 'Maseeiso said that she liked Byron for being romantic. "He compared women's beauty to the night. No one ever says that the darkness is beautiful."

"Don't you think it's beautiful right now?" Edmund asked. "Here, in the night?" She did, with the dazzle of lights and music; the blackness was a beautiful background. She liked not being able to see the mountains.

He told her of poems in every language that he knew. From all of the tribes. From poets she had never heard of before.

"That one," she said, stopping his recitation. "I like what you just said." And she quoted him quoting a dead poet: "Summon all the nations, so that we can allot the stars."

"Why do you like that one?"

"Because we should all be given a star." And he pointed to the sky, to the brightest one near his fingernail and gave it to her. Then she dared to whisper the poem about her sister near his ear.

At that moment, Eugenia approached Edmund and called out his name. She stared suspiciously at 'Maseeiso. "Do I know you?" she said, not kindly.

'Maseeiso shook her head and said nothing. Eugenia pulled Edmund out to dance–he didn't say no–and 'Maseeiso was left alone. Embarrassed, she took off and fled past the dancers, even abandoning her horse. She tripped on a rock and lost her left shoe. She let herself cry and kept running. The earth around her was lightening in the ghost-like way it did with the dawn. Soon, as the witch had warned her, the magic would fade. She sat down and cried into her skirt. All of those poems rushed through her head, yet she couldn't get Eugenia's face out of her mind–the angry eyes, the set of her chin as she led Edmund away. 'Maseeiso thought about how good Edmund smelled, and the softness of his cheek as he rested it against her own and how pleased he had seemed to talk poetry, holding her hand while they rhymed and shared snippets of their favorites, and—

"'Maseeiso." Edmund came along the path, half-running, carrying her lost shoe. "Why did you leave?" He knelt beside her. She looked at him and was amazed how deeply he looked at her.

"I thought you wanted to be with Eugenia."

"You know her?"

"I know her. I don't know why I left. Edmund, there's more I need to tell you about all of this—" She spread her hands aside, signaling the dress, the façade she wore.

At that moment the sun spooked the horizon, and she saw her shoe begin to grey.

"I am not an educated woman. All that you see is fake. Magic." She pointed towards the left-behind dance. "I don't fit in there."

He gently took her heel and slipped the second silver shoe–which was quickly dulling–on her foot. "It looks like a fit to me." As soon as the shoe was on, both began to crumble, and Edmund watched in awe–'Maseeiso with dread–when there were two piles of ash beneath 'Maseeiso's bare feet.

"Oh my God." She put her hands over face. "All this beauty is false."

Edmund took her hands. "Look at me, 'Maseeiso." She did. "Do you think when you arrived tonight I noticed your shoes? Or the dress? I'll admit, I did notice how fine your horse was." He laughed, which was in itself poetry of a new kind to 'Maseeiso. "But I noticed you. The confidence, your smile, and my God, your laughter as you danced." He touched her lips lightly with his fingers, and said softly, "It was only my luck that you were also a lover of poetry."

And before 'Maseeiso could protest, Edmund leaned over and gave her the most poetical kiss of her life.

Eugenia and her parents were shocked to come home and find 'Maseeiso gone. Ashen shoe prints led out the door, but there was nothing else. Her few possessions were left, her bed made, the house tidy. Nothing to suggest what had happened to her.

"Ran off with a man, no doubt," the stepmother sniffed, not realizing how right she might be.

"The nerve of her," Eugenia said and then burst into tears, not sad so much that her sister was gone, but that she had not captured a man at all.

The village decided she had disappeared, and they tried to inquire for a while, though no one could locate the old witch who would have been the best bet for guessing her whereabouts.

Then one day, a Saturday, when Eugenia was home, attempting to bake bread (which last week had been quite a disaster, though now she swore she was getting the hang of it), a package came in the mail. It was wrapped in a beautiful shred of fabric in a color that Eugenia had rarely set eyes on. And wrapped in this fabric was a photograph of a beautiful woman, standing outside the National University, holding a book, smiling like a radiant sunbeam.

It was a woman that Eugenia almost recognized, but not quite. From that moment on, she kept the photo pinned on the wall, above the place where 'Maseeiso–the disappeared daughter–had once slept.

Acknowledgments

I would like to thank all of my friends and family who supported the creation of this collection, who read, tore apart and praised various drafts of these stories. Thanks also to the Advanced Fiction class at the Iowa Summer Writing Festival led by Bret Anthony Johnston—you were my first critics of the first story written for this collection—thank you all for the input.

Thank you also to *A Room of Her Own Foundation* for choosing "Shades of White" as a finalist for their *Orlando Prize* in Short Fiction.

My thanks to Prudence, Steve, Janie and Nicholas Tippins for letting me stay at Shooting Star Farm for my own personal writing retreat, where many of these stories were finished.

Thanks to the Mount Holyoke Alumnae Association for the 1905 Fellowship, which provided me with the financial support to work on this collection.

Thank you to the Peace Corps for placing me in Lesotho and providing me with the opportunity to learn and be inspired by this region of Africa. A special thanks to all of my fellow PC volunteers, who were my mentors, colleagues, therapists, and most importantly, friends. And finally, thank you to all the people I met in the Mountain Kingdom...*Khotso, Pula, Nala*.

About the Author

Courtney McDermott is a native of Iowa. She has her BA in English from Mount Holyoke College and an MFA in creative writing from the University of Notre Dame. A Returned Peace Corps Volunteer in the country of Lesotho, she now teaches in Massachusetts.

CPSIA information can be obtained at www.ICGtesting.com
Printed in the USA
LVOW06s1503170415

435048LV00001B/80/P